# A VOICE WITHOUT REASON

IRENE BAHRD

*For all the good girls… and Wolf who doesn't mind calling you one "just one more time."*

## CONTENT WARNINGS

By reading this book, you may experience the following side effects:

- Wet panties.
- Desire to leave your significant other in search of your own Julian.
- Wanting to get handsy at *Hamilton*.
- Reconsidering the nickname you have for your lady bits.

*You're welcome.*

All joking aside, this is a slow-to-medium burn, instalove **romantic comedy** with on-page explicit content. It is intended for mature audiences.

Additionally, there are scenes with:

- Praise (directed at FMC)
- Brief general conversations about various kinks and BDSM

- Sexytime in public

## PLAYLIST

"I Knew I Loved You" — Savage Garden
"Enchanted" — Taylor Swift
"Meant to Be" — Bebe Rexha
"The Middle" — Zedd
"Only Wanna Be With You" — Hootie and the Blowfish
"Bubbly" — Colbie Caillat
"I Guess I'm in Love" — Clinton Kane
"Breathe" — Faith Hill
"Love Brand New" — Bob Moses
"Don't Give Up On Me" — Andy Grammer
"If I Ain't Got You" — Alicia Keys
"Thinking Out Loud" — Ed Sheeran

# 1

## BECCA

*First class upgrade? Fuck. Yes.*

I'm not typically the bougie type. Give me a budget airline, cram me into coach, and I'm happy. I love to travel, so when my airline miles added up to earn me this sweet discounted upgrade, I tapped my credit card three times and, *poof,* we were no longer in sepia-toned Kansas. I've only flown first class twice before, but I enjoy the extra perks like free drinks, early boarding, and seats that two of me could easily fit into. Sometimes you just need to treat yourself.

My boarding group is called and I make my way to the gate, scanning my ticket with a skip in my step. As I take my seat, the flight crew member takes my bag and asks, "Miss, would you like something to drink before we take off?"

"Yes, I would love a Manhattan, if it isn't too much trouble?"

"Of course not, darlin'. Make yourself comfortable, and I'll have it for you in just a few moments." She has a sweet Southern accent; I want to bottle up her kindness to save it for later. My agent could surely use some.

I'm on deadline for my fifth book, so I need to make the most of my time. On top of that, I need to edit an old manuscript so it can be sent off to voice actors for an audiobook. A lot is riding on it, so it needs to be perfect. As soon as I get home, I'm going to become a hermit and not leave my apartment until it's done. I keep my laptop bag to put under the seat in front of me and pull out my computer to dive in. Every second counts.

A few minutes later, I'm editing one of my favorite spicy scenes, where Anna is getting railed by Bryan, when my seatmate's deep voice startles me. "Mind if I use the overhead light?"

I don't look up. Instead, I wave him off so I can finish this chapter before I have to stow my electronics. He doesn't seem to mind my brushoff. *Thank goodness Mr. Seatmate understands social queues.*

"Here's your Manhattan." My new favorite person in the world is back. I lift my gaze from my computer to take it from her, but she is holding two of them.

"Thank you," Mr. Seatmate replies, taking one.

*Huh, interesting.*

I take the other. "Thank you"—I glance at her name tag —"Kristina." She smiles and heads toward the back of the plane.

"Cheers." Mr. Seatmate lifts his glass.

"Uh, yeah, cheers." We clink glasses, but I don't take a sip. I place my drink to the left of me and continue working.

A few minutes later, the pilot's announcement ends my edits of Anna's orgasm and I close my laptop. As I reach down to put it away, Mr. Seatmate leans down to put something of his own away, our shoulders bumping. "I'm sorry, go ahead."

"Sorry, thanks." I glance up and... *this guy is actually kind of hot.* I didn't get a good look at him before but now that I've ogled him a bit, I'm taking mental notes of his appearance for a character in my next book. He could be the youngest brother in a billionaire romance. Or maybe even a quarterback in a sports romcom. The possibilities are endless.

*Strong, chiseled jaw... Lush dark hair practically begging to have hands run through it... Perfect golden skin that I could only get from a professional spray tan... Sinfully beautiful light brown eyes that twinkle with mischief... Hands that belong as a necklace and put the Darcy hand flex to shame... Ruggedly handsome with an athletic build. He could throw a girl around with little effort...*

Yep, definitely going in a book. My readers are going to love him.

"Sorry, I was a bit rude earlier. I'm on deadline and need to take advantage of every moment I can. The world around me doesn't really exist right now."

"No problem, totally understand. I'm starting a new project in the next few days and will be in the same boat. Julian."

"Becca."

"So, what do you do, Becca?"

*Ugh, I hate small talk.*

"I'm a writer." I could place bets on the next question. $200 says he asks what genre I write.

"What do you write?"

*There it is.*

"Words," I reply with a smirk.

He smiles back, biting his lip. "Words?"

"Yes, I write words—on a computer, or sometimes on paper. Depends on my mood." I hate sharing that I write romance. People usually have one of two reactions. One, they judge that, because I write romance, I must not be *good enough* to write anything "more serious." Or, and possibly the worse outcome, they assume that I'm into some seriously kinky stuff. *I mean, I am, but that's none of their business…*

"Fair enough." He pauses, probably waiting for me to ask what he does. I will do no such thing; the last thing I need is to get dragged into a conversation and miss out on precious editing time after the plane takes off. I sip my Manhattan and see how long it takes for this guy to give up. "So, why are you headed to New York?"

"Stuff."

"Stuff? Let me guess: stuff and things?" he asks into his glass with a sly smile tugging at his lips.

His eyes are playful and, if I didn't know any better, I'd say this guy is flirting with me. What am I saying? Of course, he is. As a romance author, you'd think I would pick up on things like that sooner. Sadly, it's been entirely too long since I've even thought about a non-fictional man, let alone flirted with one.

He's enjoying this little banter of ours a little too much. At least he's trying to be creative. "Stuff, things, *and* places," I reply. There will be things stuffed *into* places, but that's for Anna, my protagonist, to explore if I can finish my edits this weekend.

"Ah." We are now entering an epic staredown as we both sip our drinks. He doesn't know who he's up against and breaks first. "So, Becca—who writes words and visits New York for stuff, things, and places—can you recommend any museums? I have a few days to kill before a meeting on Monday and could use some suggestions, if you've been before."

I actually live in the Upper East Side, but sure, I might as well play tourist. "I've been to a few. Depends on what you're looking for."

"I'm looking for an enjoyable weekend with intriguing company."

"I can recommend an internet search engine or an online dating platform. Either should satisfy your quest this weekend," I tease.

He lets out a soft chuckle. "True, very true. Do you enjoy non-answers?"

"Sometimes." I don't elaborate.

"Sounds like your Anna is a little more forthcoming than you are?"

I frown. "Were you peeking at my book?"

"How could I not? It looked like she was enjoying herself with Bryan. May want to rethink his name, though. Not the sexiest name to scream out in bed. It's up there with Chad." At first, I'm annoyed, but... he's not wrong. Maybe I should change it, Bryan *is* a tad dull for a romance book and I shouldn't have used it in the first place.

"Well, thank you for your notes, Julian, but I'm not sure I can change it this late in the game." I can, but I'm not going to... out of spite.

"Come on, let's workshop this. Okay, I'll start. How about Dylan?"

"Nope, used that one in a previous book."

"Ethan?"

"Done before."

"Todd?"

I shake my head. "That's worse than Bryan. I'll tell you what, I'll consider a name change, if you stop?"

"Deal." He offers his hand to shake on it. When I take it, my breath hitches.

"Did you feel that?" At first contact, a jolt radiated through my entire body.

"Feel what?" She eyes me curiously.

I squeeze her hand. "That."

"It's a handshake, Julian. Is this your first?" She might be playing coy, but I can see the surprise in her eyes. She felt it too. I don't know what it is, I'm drawn to her in a way I've never been with another woman. Holding her hand confirms it, there's something there.

I shake my head and pull my hand back. "Nevermind, you don't believe what you write."

"What's that supposed to mean?" She nervously adjusts her glasses.

"You write romance?" She nods. "Well, I'm sure you've written a scene or two where your characters share a moment of static electricity. You know, where time stops, they feel a zing course through their bodies, the air crackles between them... their breath hitches." *Thought I didn't notice?*

"I fail to see your point." She's chewing on her lip, drawing my attention to them.

"Liar. I know you felt it. Anyway, you have a new character name to come up with." I lean back in my seat and close my eyes.

"I... I'm not a liar. You must have just felt turbulence." I open one of my eyes to look at her in disbelief. We're taxiing and there hasn't been so much as a bump on the tarmac. "Okay, *fine*, there wasn't turbulence." She pulls out a tablet and begins reading. "How about Stewart? What do you think? Rolls off the tongue." She tightens her lips, attempting to hold back laughter. I do my best to school my own features, but crack first when she glances over at me.

I get a good look at her, which is a mistake. She has the most beautiful green eyes I've ever seen. I could get lost in them if I'm not careful. "You're joking right? Please tell me you're joking. Damn, I'm glad I don't have to voice female characters often. Could you imagine? *Oh, Stewie, right there?*"

Laughing, she asks, "You're a voice actor? Wait, what book are you supposed to be working on? You mentioned a meeting Monday. Oh no, please don't tell me it's mine."

"No, I'm working on a fantasy book, definitely *not* Stewart's story." That earns me another smile from her. "Would you like me to be yours?" I didn't mean for it to come out that way… *Okay, maybe a little.* She's too fun to flirt with.

"Nope, all set. I have a meeting Monday, as well, to pass off my manuscript to my new narration team. It would've just been too kismet if it was you. The narrator I'm using has never shown his face and uses a dozen pseudonyms." Despite her lack of reaction to my words, there's still a light blush dusting her cheeks. I plan to make it my life's mission to see how dark I can make it.

"May I?" I gesture to her tablet. She nods and turns it for me. It's full of markups, so this must be a copy of the book she was editing. I clear my throat before reading aloud. *"Anna's perfect supple breasts call to me and I answer. With a swipe of my tongue, I lick slow, torturous circles around each of her light pink nipples, as my hand cups her mound…* Becca, you can't say mound. It's awful."

She covers her eyes, "I know! I'm running out of synonyms for pussy. At least I didn't write 'milky folds.'" I shudder at the suggestion. *"See,* that one's the worst! What's one of the worst you've had to do for an audiobook?"

"There are so many, but the worst has to be when they call it something like 'lady garden.' There is nothing sexy about a lady garden."

Becca huffs out a laugh. "I promise, I've never used that term and never will."

I take a sip of my Manhattan. "So, what do you call yours?"

"My what?"

"You know what I'm asking, Becca," I reply, smiling into my glass.

Small lines form at the edge of her eyes and she scrunches her nose as she laughs. "I don't see how that's any of your business."

"Of course it isn't, but I'd like to know all the same."

"I'm not going to tell you, but I can say that I used it in my latest book I'm editing. If you want to know so badly, you can purchase it in three months."

*I do and I will.*

"I'll be the first in line to buy it, highlighters in hand."

"I was joking. There's no way in hell I'm giving you the title."

I pull out my phone and click on the browser. I search for Anna and Bryan, coming up empty. Maybe it's a different book? I try "Becca romance author." Nothing comes up but fluffy, closed-door romance books. She probably writes under a different name.

"What's your pen name?" I ask, not looking up from my phone.

"You just asked me what I named my vagina. You think I'm about to give away all of my secrets today?" She turns back to her tablet.

"Should I buy you dinner first?"

The flight attendant approaches. "My apologies. You'll both need to stow all electronics."

"*Shit*," Becca grumbles. "Okay, thank you." Becca places her tablet under the seat. Her shoulders slump as her head hits the headrest.

"I'm sure Anna's story will be done in time." I resist the urge to touch her. I'm pretty sure it could be deemed sexual assault if I gripped her thigh, even if it's in solidarity. I know deadlines are rough on authors, and she's probably pulling all-nighters to finish her book edits.

"Thanks. It'll work out. It always does." She finishes her drink and closes her eyes but, based on her breathing, I can tell it's just an attempt to ignore me and she's not actually resting.

As the plane takes off and, since the flirting with Becca has ceased, I'm left with my own thoughts. I know nothing about her, but she is the most intriguing woman I've ever met. I've done nothing but hit on her since the moment I sat down, yet she never shied away from it, meeting me with a fun, flirtatious energy.

The flight from California will give me more than enough time to get to know her. I know the moment she's able to take out her laptop, her faux nap will come to an end, and she won't be able to ignore me.

Our seatbelt signs click off with the familiar ding, as the flight attendant announces that we are able to use electronics in airplane mode. As predicted, I've never seen someone move so fast. I can't help but chuckle.

I sit back further, in hopes of getting a glimpse at her book title or pen name.

**Delivery of Fate [Audio Notes]**

Just like that, I'll be able to find her. I access the in-flight WiFi and open my browser. "Delivery of Fate romance book" yields only one possible result: Merlot Bennet. *Merlot Bennet?* Fuck. She's not just any romance author, she's a top ten best selling author. Her last two books took off, making her a household name synonymous with "spicy contemporary romance." Here I thought she might be some quirky indie author, but I'm way out of my element here.

I pull up an author spotlight interview and, sure enough, it's her. Same beautiful clusters of freckles dusting her nose, bright emerald green eyes, and dark chestnut brown hair. I didn't recognize her with her purple-rimmed glasses on—like some kind of Clark Kent for smutty books.

I turn toward her with a smirk. "So, *Merlot*, how is Anna and Bryan's love story coming along?"

She sucks in a breath and refuses to meet my gaze. "They're doing great. I really should change his name. You know what would be a great name to call out in bed…" She does a 'find and replace' in her document and switches out Bryan for Julian. She bites her lip and finally looks at me, even if it's just the corner of her eye.

I lean in and lower my voice. "You should switch it back. Unless you plan on finding out for yourself what it's like to call out my name in bed."

"Too bad we'll be parting ways after this flight and we'll never find out." She hits the call button for the flight attendant and adds, "Question is, will you be moaning Becca or Merlot while you're fucking yourself tonight?"

Fuck, I like her. "Or, hear me out, you could let me take you to dinner, then end the night in my hotel room where we'll find out, once and for all, how my name sounds after a few orgasms."

She presses 'undo' on the laptop, switching Julian back to Bryan. "Guess we'll never know, will we?"

*Maybe not today, but we most definitely will, my Becca.*

A flight attendant approaches. Becca asks for a refill on her drink she's barely touched. When they leave, I ask, "Who do you have narrating for you?"

Becca initially ignores my question, but eventually answers with a sigh, "John Barker."

John's great and hard to book. "Why aren't you more excited about working with him?"

"His voice doesn't quite fit my character. I need him a bit more… growly."

I nod but otherwise don't reply, letting her get back to her writing. I pull up my email app and type out a quick message to my agent before diving into some work of my own.

# 3

## BECCA

"Miss, you need to put your laptop away for landing."

*Shit.*

I still have edits to make on chapter 33, where Bryan goes down on Anna and gives her a third orgasm in the scene. It's feeling a little 'rinse and repeat' and I need something to liven it up.

Julian spent most of the flight working as well. He has some sort of audio mixer open as he takes notes in his leather bound notebook. I don't know much about him and now is as good a time as any to do a little sleuthing. I stow my laptop and open my audiobook app on my phone. I search for 'Julian' under narrators, only finding two results that aren't children's books:

*Julian Evans*

*Julian Kincade*

Since this Kincade fellow only does nonfiction, my seat-mate must be Julian Evans. I click on his name and scroll the various titles he's worked on, finding mostly fantasy and a few thrillers. I click on one that has duet narration and listen to the sample file.

His voice is sultry but commanding. I think back to earlier, when he read a paragraph of mine out loud, and realize he would be a much better fit than John for my book. I need someone who can make panties wet and hearts race; I'm worried John won't be able to pull it off.

Distracted by looking out the window as we descend, and listening to one of Julian's audiobooks about a were-wolf shifter professing his feelings for a vampire princess, I'm startled when he takes my hand in his. He interlocks our fingers and I freeze.

*Maybe flying makes him nervous? No, that can't be it. Do I pull away and embarrass him? Kind of a bitch move, seeing as I don't really care…*

There's still a weird, kinetic energy between us—the feeling romance books are made of. I've written about it a hundred times before, but, admittedly, had never experienced it myself. I don't know this man, other than his name, the sound of his voice describing a werewolf shifter in great detail, and that he has no issue asking inappropriate questions of a stranger.

Before I can even decide how to react, he pulls his hand away quickly. "I'm so sorry, I… *fuck*. I didn't mean to…"

"It's okay, I figured you might just have issues flying or something."

"No, worse." He shakes his head with a chuckle. "My girlfriend and I broke up a week ago, and it's kind of a habit. I forgot who I was next to for a moment. We… we were together for three years."

"Oh, I'm sorry. So, what did you do to get dumped?"

Julian quirks an eyebrow at me. "How do you know it was *me* who was dumped? I could have dumped her, you know."

I snort-laugh. *Actually snort.* "Yeah, okay."

"You don't believe me?" He asks with a smirk.

Shifting in my seat to sit up taller, I double down. "No, I don't. You wouldn't *accidentally* be holding a stranger's hand if you were the one who dumped her. If I had to guess, I'd say the breakup was work-related, or"—I gasp, clutching my chest—"you're a cheater." I fail to keep my amusement contained.

"Wrong on both accounts. She cheated on me."

"Oh, shit. I'm sorry, I didn't mean—" *Man, I'm an asshole.*

"With my brother."

I narrow my eyes; there's something familiar and all-too-convenient about that. I figure it out a moment later. It's part of the plot of *Delivery of Fate*. He must have been reading over my shoulder again.

"Out with it. What's the real reason?"

"She did cheat on me, just not with my brother."

There's so much hurt in his eyes when he looks away. They were together so long, it must still sting to think about.

I place my hand on his. "I'm sorry. It's never fun to be cheated on. I shouldn't have assumed."

Turning his hand over, he holds mine again, this time squeezing once and not letting go. "You can make up for your blunder by having dinner with me."

"That's the third time you've asked."

"And the third time you avoided giving me an answer," he replies with a wink.

"Do I want to go to dinner with a broken-hearted man who has no issue asking a stranger what she calls her pussy? Sounds like a terrible idea."

"Really? Because I think it's the best idea I've ever had."

---

So, apparently, I'm a woman who goes to dinner with heartbroken men who have no filter.

"What was your inspiration for *Vacation with the Enemy*?"

I eye him suspiciously. "How do you know so much about my books?"

He takes a sip of his Manhattan and explains, "Everyone knows who you are. Your book made number one for e-book sales and stayed there for three months. Not bad for an author with a small backlist."

No matter how popular my books get, I have severe imposter syndrome—constantly feeling like I'm not a real author and that this is all a joke. "Have you read my work? It's not exactly Pulitzer Prize material."

"Who needs a Pulitzer when nearly every woman in America has read your books?" He shrugs. "Even I read one."

My eyes widen. My first instinct is to ask what he thought, but I can't bring myself to say anything. *What if he hated it? No, if he hated it, he wouldn't have brought it up.*

As if reading my thoughts, Julian reaches across the table and takes my hand. "It was good." When he pulls back, I'm acutely aware that I'm starting to enjoy his innocent touches a little too much.

"Thank you." I take a few long drinks of my Manhattan, hoping it will prolong the silence.

"I didn't think to ask earlier, but where do you live? I couldn't find it while internet stalking you earlier." He takes a bite of his chicken parmigiana, awaiting my answer.

"In an apartment."

He chuckles. "Ah, I should've known I'd receive a non-answer. Well, perhaps if I share, then you will. I live in Temecula, wine country, about ninety minutes from LA. Your turn."

"I never agreed to your terms. I live in… the United States."

Julian continues eating with the most adorable boyish grin spreading ear to ear. "I expected nothing less."

After a few more Manhattans and entirely too much flirting, the check comes and I try to snatch it before him. I know from my own internet deepdive that he's well off enough to own a vineyard in California. Not a huge surprise—he was in first class with me, after all. *Maybe voice acting is just a hobby?* But my paying will ensure this wasn't truly a date. I could even write it off as a business expense if need be. Unfortunately, he's quicker.

"I'll make you a deal," Julian says, resting his elbows on the table and smirking at me. "I'll let you pay, if you agree to go out with me again this weekend."

"Or, I can lie, pay the bill, and go home—never to be seen or heard from again." I finish my drink and am now feeling a little buzzed.

*Ok, maybe more than a little. Maybe I should go back to his hotel? When was the last time I got laid? Besides, it's not like I'll ever see him again.*

"Home? So, you're a New Yorker?"

*Shit.* "I meant to my own hotel."

"Do you live here in the city, *Merlot?*"

Trying my best to smother a smile, I sigh, "Yes, I live in New York."

"Then, let me see to it that you get home safe." The twinkle in his eyes is unmistakable. He's a whole package of trouble—incredibly attractive and the biggest flirt I have ever met.

"Maybe another time. I still have work to do tonight." It's not a lie, I really do have another two hours, at least, of work to do, probably more after the Manhattans.

"You have your laptop with you, so let's go find a late

night coffee shop and we can both get some work done," he offers.

"Julian, you are relentless."

"Yes. Yes, I am. I enjoy spending time with you, so if you want to spend that time working, then so be it." He shrugs and slides his credit card into the leather folder, setting it on the edge of the table.

His answer takes me by surprise. I was certain he just wanted to get in my pants. I mean, he *definitely* does, but I also feel like his answer is genuine, and we have some sort of inexplicable connection.

Going against all reason, I agree to coffee. "Sure."

---

"Okay, what if I change it to Stewart and make this a romcom instead?" I'm on my second double espresso con panna and have accepted that sleep isn't in my future any time soon. I'll stay up until tomorrow night if I have to; my book isn't going to edit itself.

"You're not changing your entire story. Maybe kill off the brother and Bryan has to get revenge?"

Julian's made me laugh so hard these past few hours that my stomach hurts. "This isn't a thriller or romantic suspense. No, I feel like it's in a good place, I just need to put a few last minute sprinkles of love on it before I meet with John."

He yawns. "Becca, listen to me, it's fine as-is."

I check the time on my phone. "Shit, it's 2:30! I'm so sorry, I shouldn't have kept you out this late."

"Nonsense. There's nowhere I'd rather be. I just need a nap and we can continue this little date of ours. I checked in at the hotel on my app, looks like they upgraded me to a suite. Want to come by for a bit? Little power nap before breakfast?" He begins picking up trash and my empty espresso mug—the international sign for 'we're leaving.'

"I shouldn't."

"But you want to. I promise I won't be on my best behavior."

I chuckle. "I think it's supposed to be: I promise I'll be on my best behavior."

"That would be a lie." Julian gets up to toss the trash and gives the barista our mugs. When he returns, instead of sitting across from me like before, he takes the seat next to me. I close my laptop and face him with a wide smile. He bites his bottom lip, drawing my attention to them. "Becca, I'm going to kiss you now, and you're going to let me."

"I am?"

He leans in slowly and glides his hand into my hair. "Yeah. You are."

I close the distance. Just as my lips are about to reach his, the barista behind me clears his throat. "Sorry, we're closing up. You know the drill, you don't have to go home, but you can't stay here."

Shutting my eyes tight, I shake my head and wince. "Yeah, thanks, friend."

Julian chuckles and, in an instant, his lips are on mine. After an evening full of flirting and anticipation, I can't help but moan at first contact. He teases with his tongue and I open for him willingly. He tastes like black coffee and the blueberry scone he had earlier, and I'm never going to be able to look at scones again without thinking of him. His kisses aren't urgent, they're sensual and playful—a dangerous combination.

"You sure you don't want to stay with me tonight?" he mutters against my lips.

As we break away, I reluctantly reply, "I'm sure, but if you're ever in New York again, look me up. I might change my mind."

He stands and takes my hand. "You better believe I'm going to take you up on that. Who knows, maybe that'll be sooner rather than later."

We head outside and order separate ride shares. His phone pings with a text or email and he checks it. He glances at me with a smirk, replies to whatever message he received, and stuffs it back in his pocket as his ride arrives first.

"Thank you for tonight, Julian."

He wraps me in his arms and kisses me softly. "Pleasure is all mine, my Becca."

"Have a… wonderful life? Seeing as we'll probably never meet again and all."

*Maybe I should go to his hotel? This whole thing could be the perfect meet cute in my next novel, I could see it through…*

As he steps into the car, he pauses. "Monday."

"What?" I ask with a frown. He gets in and closes the door without another word. "Julian? What's Monday?" I shout at the car.

It drives off and once in my own rideshare, I receive an email from my agent.

---

**To**: Merlot Bennet

**From**: Cassandra Wilson

**Subject**: Change in MMC Narration

Becca,

Sorry to email you in the middle of the night, but your publisher made some drastic changes yesterday and I just confirmed it all now. They are pulling John from *Delivery of Fate* and replacing him with another narrator. I don't know much about him, but I'll send over a few samples of his work, and if you hate him I'll renegotiate the contract.

Message me over the weekend with any questions.

See you Monday!

Cassie

# 4

# JULIAN

**To**: Andre Stark

**From**: Julian Evans

**Subject**: Delivery of Fate by Merlot Bennet

Andre,

I'll do it for free, just make it happen.

Regards,

Julian

---

**To**: Julian Evans

**From**: Andre Stark

**Subject**: RE: Delivery of Fate by Merlot Bennet

Julian,

Merlot Bennet is kind of a big deal. I don't know if I can make that kind of miracle happen. You don't have much experience in romance, especially with on-page explicit content. For free? We can talk more about this when you land in NY. I need more details.

Best,

Andre

---

**To**: Andre Stark

**From**: Julian Evans

**Subject**: RE: RE: Delivery of Fate by Merlot Bennet

Andre,

I want it. Give her whatever she wants. I'll waive all commission and give it to her, if it means I get to work with her.

Regards,

Julian

---

**To**: Julian Evans

**From**: Andre Stark

**Subject**: RE: RE: RE: Delivery of Fate by Merlot Bennet

Green light. It's yours.

Attached is a copy of the e-contract. Sign it and you're the new narrator.

-Andre

Sent from my phone

---

I haven't been able to wipe the smile off my face for the last three days. Not only will I be narrating for Becca, but her publisher insisted that she be present for the recordings. My inexperience is working to my advantage. Two words: *forced proximity*.

I'm not normally so forward with women, but there's something special about Becca that makes me want to spend time with her and get to know her. One look at her and all common sense went out the fucking window. I hope she's not too upset with me taking the contract out from under John—she said herself he wasn't quite *growly* enough.

Our meeting is in five minutes, so I'm taking a breather in the men's room, bracing myself on the sink and questioning how much I overstepped. She can't be *that* mad, right? I just had to guarantee that I'd see her again and, well, I panicked. It made the most sense at the time when I emailed Andre on the plane.

When I enter the conference room, Becca and her agent are sitting at the table alongside a man and woman I haven't met before. She must be the female narrator. I've been so consumed with seeing my beautiful stranger again that I didn't even look into who was voicing Anna.

I can't take my eyes off Becca as I take my seat; she's beyond captivating. When she spots me, neither of us look away, even as her agent, Cassandra, starts the meeting and introduces everyone at the table. I'm hardly listening. Have Becca's eyes always been so intensely green? They're sparkling, even though she looks less than pleased to see me.

Breaking eye contact feels like I've been drenched by a bucket of ice water. Becca finally addresses the group. "Thank you all for being here. I appreciate your flexibility with these last minute changes. To ensure we all have the best experience, I'd like to ask Julian and Caroline to run a few lines from chapter 23. I've printed out copies and highlighted what you're responsible for in Anna's POV."

We ruffle through the papers Becca provided, and Caroline begins, "*Julian, I can explain...*" She continues thumbing through the pages. "Wait, the character's name is Julian? I thought it was Bryan. Isn't *your* name Julian?"

I try to resist laughing, but a chuckle escapes me. Becca replies, "Changes were made over the weekend before I knew we had a new narrator. It's purely coincidental, I assure you."

*Oh, my Becca, you are such a liar.*

Caroline clears her throat and starts at the top, "*Julian, I can explain. He didn't mean anything to me.*"

*"He's my brother, Anna. How could you do this to——"*

"I've heard enough," Becca says coldly. "I'll be in touch."

She begins to stand and I continue, "How could you do this to me? What we had was special; it transcended time and space. You're the most incredible woman I've ever known…"

"That's not in my book," Becca says quietly.

I stand and round the table until I reach her. "You're right." I lower my voice. "But does it make it any less true?"

Becca opens and closes her mouth a few times, searching for an answer before she chooses to address the team, "Can we have a moment? Is there a free office where I can discuss something with Mr. Evans in private?"

"Turn left and the second door on the right," Cassandra says, clearly confused and concerned. Becca turns on her heel and walks out of the room. I follow.

As soon as we're in the office, she lays into me. "What the *fuck* do you think you're doing? I had one of the top narrators in the industry scheduled and you think you can just waltz in here and… what's your deal?"

"I had to see you."

"Bull fucking shit. You put this in motion when we were on the plane. You're not even taking a commission? Are you kidding me? I don't want your money. I want the best damn narrator for the job. You think you can tell their story better than John could have?" Becca begins pacing. "I got lucky with two of my books. If the narration isn't perfect, I risk bad reviews that don't just reflect on you, they reflect on *me*, as an author. This story is very personal to me. What were you thinking? Is this because I wouldn't sleep with you?"

I stop her in her tracks, one hand on each of her shoulders. "No, absolutely not. This has nothing to do with sex, Becca. I promise you, I would never have requested this job if I couldn't do it. Tell me what you need and I'll deliver, I promise you that."

"Why should I listen to you? I barely know you."

"You know what, just put the book aside for a moment. Something happened between us a few days ago that neither of us can explain. Have you spent every waking moment thinking about it? Fuck, I know I have. Why else would you change your character's name to mine?"

A part of my soul left my body when I got in that car to my hotel and didn't return until I saw her today. I don't know what it is about her, but I want, no, I *need* to be with her. Whatever that looks like.

"I changed it to fuck with you."

I scoff. "Such a fucking liar." I snake my arm around Becca, pulling her to me until her mouth is a breath away. She whimpers as our bodies collide and I know damn well she wants me as much as I want her. I risk everything and kiss her brutally, tasting and teasing her mouth like it's mine to explore. A risk worth taking.

My luck runs out when there's a knock at the door, breaking whatever spell we're under. "Merlot, are you doing okay in there?"

"Yeah, thanks," Becca calls, then lowers her voice so only I can hear. "Don't make me regret this." She turns and walks out.

## 5

## BECCA

My heels click loudly on the marble floor as I storm back down the hallway. Julian's footsteps are fast approaching, but I don't let him catch up to get another word in. I reenter the conference room and take a seat, doing my best to not let that kiss affect me. I didn't work this hard for everything to be thrown away because of some hot guy.

"Mr. Evans will be resuming the narration for Julian," I insist, pocketing all of my emotions.

I should really change the name back to Bryan, but it's the least I can do to make his life difficult. It took pulling some strings over the weekend to get approval for Julian over Bryan, but thankfully they agreed that Anna moaning Bryan wasn't going to turn anyone on.

*Even if I was the one moaning it not so long ago.*

I pack up my bag and head for the door. "Oh, and I'll need the contract adjusted. I won't be present for Mr. Evans' recording sessions."

My publisher can suck it. There's no way in hell I'm going to sit in a recording booth for hours on end with that man.

I make my way to the elevator, but Cassie stops me before I can get in. "Your publisher isn't budging on this, since he's new to romance and smutty books. You'll have to be there."

"No. Absolutely not. Pull the contract if you have to, but I'm not going to be forced to hear Julian say '*you take me so well*' over and over again, until he gets it right."

Cassie smirks. "I mean, at least he's not hard on the eyes. There are worse guys I could put in that booth to call you a good girl and describe in great detail how they'd ravish your body."

"This is my career on the line. I don't have time to babysit an inexperienced narrator. Give me one reason I should use his voice over John's." *It better not be because he's hot.*

"It's all—"

"Hey, can we talk?" Julian's deep purr comes from behind me. The elevator door opens and I refuse to acknowledge him as the three of us step in. I deliberately stand on the other side of Cassie, practically holding my breath.

We remain standing there in silence down the twenty-three floors. I've never been so thankful for elevator music in my life. The ding, followed by doors opening, has me sprinting out of the elevator.

"Becca, wait. Slow down." Unfortunately, I don't get far when he reaches for me, gripping my arm and spinning me in place. "Please." His low voice sends a shiver down my spine.

Cassie gives me a knowing look but continues to head toward the exit. I need to be careful what I say around him now that we're working together. There's explicit content in the contracts that could screw both of us.

My eyes narrow. "Fine, you want to talk? Then talk."

Julian looks around until he spots two unoccupied leather seats on the other side of the lobby. He takes my hand but I shrug out of his hold as we head over to sit down. He claims a chair, but I stand, arms crossed.

"Please, have a seat. This won't take long."

My jaw ticks. "Then, I'll stand. What do you need to talk about?"

He hunches over and rests his elbows on his knees. With a deep breath, he asks, "What do I need to do to make this up to you? I'm sorry, I shouldn't have emailed Andre on the plane. I was—"

"Did you do this as a PR stunt as soon as you found out who I was? Fuck this. I'm out, Julian."

"No." He stands and takes a step toward me. "I didn't care if you were an up-and-coming self-pub author or *the* Merlot Bennet. I wanted your book because I wanted to spend time with you. Nothing more. I'll even narrate under a pseudonym if you want. I just"—Julian rakes his hand through his hair—"I wanted a chance to spend time with you and this seemed like my best option."

"*Shit*," I mutter. "You thought messing with my career was your best option? So, what now? You got the book and now will have to spend countless hours reciting how Anna is getting fucked over and over and *over* again. Happy?"

Julian takes another step toward me. "Yes. I am actually."

*I should've just slept with him. Maybe then he wouldn't have tried to fuck up my audiobook.*

"I know you've heard my work. I can do this and I'll record thirty takes of me saying '*that's my good girl*' to get it right, if that's what you want." He tucks a strand of hair behind my ear and cups my neck, stroking my cheek. "Let me do this."

I sigh into his touch… until reality sets in. I like him, that's undeniable, but he crossed a line.

"You got the job." I take a step back. "But whatever this is between us is done. I'll see you tomorrow for a readthrough. Have a good day, Mr. Evans."

---

"I can't believe it! What an asshole." Amanda shakes her head before downing her shot of tequila and chasing it with a beer.

After the shit day I've had, I called one of my favorite author friends for drinks and a debrief. Amanda hit it big with a viral social media video—the equivalent of winning the lottery in the indie author world. She landed a huge book deal with a major publisher and, since then, the two of us have traded off taking the number one spot with online retailers. If anyone understands what I'm dealing with, it's her. What started out as one drink at a restaurant bar quickly turned into four. At this rate, we'll need to go dancing after this to sober up before heading home.

I take my shot, savoring the burn with no chaser. "Asshole," I echo. "The worst part? *Julian's* voice is actually perfect for *Julian*." I fucked myself. I definitely need to change it back to Bryan… or literally anything else.

Amanda signals for another round. "Let me have a listen." I hand her my wireless earbuds out of my purse and press play on one of the audiobooks on my app. A minute or two later, her eyes are wide as she takes out the earbuds. "He's actually good, Becs. Can you imagine what he'll sound like when he has to groan or growl into her pussy?"

I'm unable to help the laugh that escapes me. "This is a nightmare! He's hot, too. Did I tell you he's hot? And flirty. He's been hitting on me since the moment we met. He actually asked what I call my lady bits." She chokes on her beer. "Right? Who does that?"

*That one I'm taking to the grave.*

Our shots arrive and we toss them back quickly, finishing with limes between our teeth. "Okay, let's settle up and head two doors down to the hotel bar. There are *always* men there who are hot as fuck and only in town for business. Perfect for a no strings attached evening." She wiggles her eyebrows.

"I haven't had sex since…"

"Bryan," we say in unison.

"See, Becs! It's meant to be."

---

We're probably the youngest people here. A few silver foxes bought us drinks, but I have no desire to go upstairs with someone who likely needs a little blue pill to have a good time. I'll never yuck someone's yum, but an age gap romance is not for me.

The man to Amanda's left is incredibly attractive and most definitely interested in her, so I busy myself reading a book on my e-reader. If I can't have a real life book-worthy romance right now, I may as well read about a sexy man doing delicious things to a woman in a first person point of view.

Engrossed in a scene, a delicious voice startles me. "Well, isn't this a pleasant surprise."

I fumble my e-reader and it slides over the bar, clinking against various alcohol bottles on its way to the floor. "Shit. Julian, what are you doing here?"

"I was about to ask the same thing, *Merlot*."

Amanda swivels in her seat. "Did someone just say… Why, hello there." She drinks him in, then gives me a pointed look.

"Julian, this is Amanda. Amanda, Julian. Of all the bars in all the hotels, it had to be here." I sigh in defeat.

She offers her hand. "Pleasure to meet you, Julian. I've heard so much about you."

"Is that so?" Julian asks with a smirk. He signals to the bartender and orders himself a Manhattan.

*Of course he had to drink the same thing as me...*

I finish mine in a few quick gulps and toss down $40. I lean in to Amanda and keep my voice low. "Well, I better head out before another audiobook contract of mine is hijacked. See you Thursday for lunch?" Amanda nods, her attention mostly on the tall drink of water next to her. As I get up, I wrap my arm around her from behind and press a kiss to her cheek. "Have fun, girly."

She pats my arm and I release it as she whispers, "You were right about him... *hot.*" I groan, rolling my eyes. "See you for lunch, babe."

I try to move past Julian but he catches me by the waist. "Leaving so soon?"

"Early morning," I lie.

His lips brush my ear, causing the hairs to rise on my neck. I hate and love the effect he has on me. "One drink?"

"No good can come from it." My gaze meets his as he steps back. "Are you staying here?" I ask and he nods in reply. I should make it my mission to not come within twenty blocks of this hotel as long as I know Julian's in New York. "Goodnight, Julian."

I only make it three steps when he asks, "Why didn't you change it back to Bryan?"

Glancing back at him, I reply, "Always wanted to know

what it would be like to call out 'Julian' in bed. This is the closest I'll ever get to it."

His boyish grin couldn't be wider. I shouldn't flirt with him. I shouldn't keep him on as my narrator. I shouldn't want him. Yet… here we are.

# 6

## JULIAN

I can't keep my eyes off her as she walks away. Becca turns back once and... *fuck it.* I take out a $20 from my wallet, slap it onto the bar, and run after her.

"Good luck, Romeo," her friend calls after me.

"Becca, wait." She doesn't stop, so I pick up my pace. When I reach her, I catch her hand and pull her toward me. "I have an idea. Do you trust me?" She looks down at our hands and back up at me, but doesn't pull away.

"No," she replies flatly.

"Will you at least hear me out?"

With a sigh, she concedes, "Sure."

"Come on, I'll explain on the way." I begin guiding us toward the elevator. We barely make it a dozen steps before she pulls her hand from mine, ending the little adventure we were about to embark on. "I have my equipment upstairs. I want to record a few chapters for you and get your feedback," I explain.

Becca crosses her arms. "Record them and send me the files."

"Real-time feedback. I want to know what I can fix in the moment."

"I swear, Julian, if this is some weird elaborate ruse to get me naked…"

I let out a hearty laugh. "I mean, if you want to be naked, I certainly wouldn't complain." My eyes wander halfway down to her chest but I catch myself and quickly look back to her emerald green eyes. "Every-thing is set up in the living room of my suite."

"No improv like you pulled when we were in the meeting?"

"I promise." I offer my hand. "Come on. It'll be fun."

---

I can't believe she actually agreed. Shrugging off my jacket, I toss it onto the back of the closest chair and grab two bottles of water from the mini fridge. I've been chasing this woman since the moment I sat down next to her on the plane and I'm not giving up until I've won her over. The first step is to get her to forgive me for the stunt I pulled. If I play my cards right, we'll have a chance to get to know one another better and, if I'm lucky, she might even let me take her on a real date.

Becca pulls up a copy of the audiobook notes on my computer. "Where do you want to start?"

After reading through her book over the weekend, I know I'm in for a rough few weeks. Between the roller-coaster of emotions these characters have and the on-page sex, it's going to be quite a range for me to master.

"How about chapter 12?" A sly smirk spreads across my face.

Her eyes widen and she replies, "Oh, um… sure."

I take the computer from her, scroll to chapter 12, and prep the rest of my equipment. "You'll need to sit closer if you want to listen in."

"I can hear just fine from where I'm at, thank you."

"Becca, sit next to me. I won't make a pass at you. You have to listen through the headphones to have an idea of what this will sound like once recorded." I offer a set of my headphones to her. With a sigh, she gets up from the opposite chair to sit next to me on the couch. "Can you do Anna's part to help with pacing?"

"I don't record audiobooks. I'm an author. I know what I want from a narrator, but I don't want to do it myself. I want someone else to do it for me." She laughs nervously. "That, uh, came out wrong. You know what I mean."

*Oh, I absolutely do. But I want to play the long game here.*

"You don't have to add inflection, just read the words on the page for me."

Reluctantly, she starts reading.

**Anna**: *We spent two hot nights together and now I have to work for him. Every time Julian walks by, my stomach twists and I* *can't catch my breath. Pulling me from my thoughts, he taps my desk and demands.*

**Julian**: *"Anna, can I see you in my office?"*

**Anna**: *I nod and swallow hard, following him down the hall. I wait in the doorway as he rounds his desk and sits in his large leather chair.*

**Julian**: *"Have a seat."*

**Anna**: *I stay rooted in place.*

**Julian**: *"Sit, Anna."*

**Anna**: *I take a deep breath and sit in the chair opposite him.*

**Julian**: *"Since we're working together, I need to make one thing clear, kitten."*

**Anna**: *I swallow hard.*

**Julian**: *"I want you."*

Becca takes off the headphones abruptly. "I'm sorry. I can't do this." I pause the recording and remove my own, watching her stand and grab her purse. "You're right; it'll be good to have you do Bryan's part."

Now that I have her here, I don't want her to leave. Not like this. I don't even want to seduce her, I just enjoy spending time with her. I chose that scene in the hopes that she would hear my words, not Bryan/Julian, but it seems to have backfired epically.

"Hey, what's wrong?" I stand and beat her to the door. "The recording is fine. If you're worried about the quality, I can—"

"No." She blows out a deep breath and looks away, her voice soft. "It's not the recording; it's the book. I should go."

I tilt her chin to look at me. "Your book is fine. What's this about?"

"I shouldn't have let it get picked up. Have you looked at my backlist?" I shake my head. "Look at the original date of *Delivery of Fate.*" Becca takes out her phone and pulls up a photo on her social media feed of her book with a different cover. I take the phone and peer at the date. It was self-published three years ago.

"Was this your debut novel?"

She shakes her head once and takes the phone back. "Second, but scrubbed and rebranded for re-release."

I've been a narrator for many years and have had the pleasure of working with a variety of traditional and indie authors. The one thing they almost always have in common is their first few novels tell a story that's important enough to make them finally take the leap to write and publish in the first place. Thinking about Anna and Bryan's story, it must mean a lot to her. Maybe Bryan was an ex? Maybe Anna is a friend? I need to find out.

"Who's Bryan to you? Did you cheat on him with his brother?" I ask in jest.

"I should go," she replies quietly

Shit, I read this wrong. "Did he cheat on you?" Her eyes fill with unshed tears. *Fuck.* "Becca, I'm so sorry."

"No, don't apologize. It's my own fault for writing the book in the first place. We worked together. He wasn't my boss or anything, but some of what happened in the book wasn't just 'inspired by' actual events." Becca wipes the corner of her eye. "Writing it and hearing it are two very different experiences."

"Come here." I take her in my arms, unsure how she'll react. She gives in and embraces me back, giving me hope that she might be just as comfortable in my arms as I am in hers.

"I'm fine, really. It was just too much for me to listen to after a few drinks tonight."

I press my lips to the top of her head. "He was a fucking idiot."

"Yeah, well, he's living his best life right now with Big Boob Brenda and—"

"And you're one of the biggest authors in the world. He deserves Brenda, he doesn't deserve you." I hold her tighter and can't help breathing in her jasmine-scented hair.

She chuckles. "You don't know me. For all you know, Brenda is pretty great."

*Not a chance, my Becca. You're extraordinary.*

"What did you say?"

Fuck, I think I said that out loud. I clear my throat. "Just said, 'not a chance.' Are you hungry? Up for grabbing a bite?"

Becca looks up at me, her eyes darting between my mouth and my eyes. "I should probably eat something, but you don't have to—"

I close the distance between us, cutting off her words with my lips on hers. I know I have the worst timing, and she's vulnerable, but I haven't wanted to do anything else since I kissed her the first time outside the coffee shop… and impulsively in the office.

"I shouldn't be kissing you," she mutters against my lips. She's right, even as she returns my kiss. Being under contract is now a conflict of interest, but I couldn't care less. I want her more than I've wanted anything else in my life. If they pull me from the project for this, so be it.

"You absolutely should." We slowly break apart and I take her hand, brushing a chaste kiss to her knuckles. "Come on, I know just the place."

# 7

## BECCA

"New York pizza is superior. How can you even think about comparing a deep-dish disaster to this delicious foldable goodness?" I take a bite and let out an exaggerated moan. "*So good.*"

"This place just came recommended by a few people and I've been wanting to give it a try all weekend. It's good, but I've had better." Julian shrugs and resumes eating.

"Doubtful. But I've been meaning to ask you, are you going on Saturday?"

Frowning, he asks, "What's Saturday?"

"Book Love Convention. I know a lot of narrators will be there, I just assumed you were going."

"I was supposed to be back in California, so I didn't get a ticket to attend or a table. But I'm here with you, so it seems life has other plans for me here in New York." There's a twinkle in his eyes as he smirks.

*Man, this guy is trouble.*

"It's sold out, but I'll be sure to send selfies with your favorite authors," I say with a wink. I shouldn't be enjoying flirting this much, but it's been a while since I've had the attention of a hot man like this. It feels good, too good.

We finish our pizza and this little impromptu date feels like it's coming to an end. The realization makes me unexpectedly sad.

*No, this isn't a date. We're just two people eating pizza.*

He moves me to the inside of the sidewalk and takes my hand as we walk back to his hotel.

*Is this a date?*

This whole thing would make for an amazing plot of a book. As soon as I'm home, I'm going to voice memo myself to save the idea for later.

"What's on your mind?"

His words pull me from my thoughts. "Oh, I just have a story idea I'm trying to flush out."

"Care to share? I'll sign an NDA." His dimples are on full display. I'm sure they have quite the effect on the ladies back home. Shaking my head and biting my lip, I resist the urge to tell him. "Fair enough." We stop in front of his hotel. "Well, this is me."

He didn't invite me up. Maybe I was wrong about him and he's just a big flirt. I take a deep breath and pivot my emotions. "I should check the bar and see if Amanda is still there."

"And if she's not?" he asks hopefully.

"Then, I'm going to bed. I need to wrap up my work in progress so I can start a new book idea I have." I don't do well with too many projects on deck, they start to bleed into each other if I try to write more than one book at a time.

"Why not come to bed with me? To sleep, of course."

I can't help but chuckle. "You're the same man that said he couldn't promise that he'd be on his best behavior."

Julian steps closer, pulling me to him by the small of my back. "Who in their right mind would want to?" His hand glides into my hair as he kisses me softly.

*Definitely a date.*

"I should check to see if she's still here and head home," I say with a sigh.

"Well, aren't you the voice of reason."

"And you, Julian, are a voice without reason."

---

"I think I like him." I recount the story of last night with Julian over coffee with Amanda. He didn't invite me upstairs a second time, but I definitely wanted him to. He's wearing me down. I shouldn't date him; it could get messy... like it did with Bryan, and I don't know if I could put myself through that again.

"Becs, I say this with love: fuck the hot narrator. Get it out of your system. He doesn't live here and probably doesn't want anything serious." She shrugs and blows on her steaming chai.

I groan. Not only are there legal implications, this feels all too familiar. "I can't have sex with someone I'm working with."

"He's not Bryan. Just ask him to practice his vocal exercises on your clit. I saw how he was looking at you; he'd totally be into it." She offers me a piece of her scone, but I decline.

Looking around, I whisper-shout, "Will you keep it down? It's 9am. No one wants to hear about tonguing clits this early in the morning."

Amanda just laughs, waving off my concern. Both of our phones chime with email notifications. Opening the app, I check mine.

---

**To**: Merlot Bennet

**From**: Book Love New York

**Subject**: New Authors and Narrators Added

We are pleased to announce the following authors and narrators have been added to our line-up this Saturday:

*Layla Thorne (Author)*

*Julian Kincade (Narrator)*

*Amanda Storm (Author)*

Please see the attached updated map, as some table placements have changed since our previous email.

See you Saturday!

Denise Johnson

Book Love New York

---

"You're coming to Book Love?" I show her my phone.

"Yeah, I almost forgot to sign up. They squeezed me in at the last minute. You and me, we're a big deal, kid. Of course they gave me a table when I asked," she says with a wink.

I chuckle. "You were the one who told me to go in the first place! How did you forget?"

She shrugs and goes back to scrolling her phone. I pull up the new map; it looks like they placed Julian Kincade next to my table and Layla across from me. Amanda is stuck on the other side of the large room. I adore Layla, but she lives on the other side of the country from me, so we don't get to talk as often. I'm excited to see her and catch up.

"Did you see the map? I'm next to a non-fiction narrator. He's about to have a rude awakening when he sees my banner with a half-naked man on it," I giggle. Male models for book covers and promotion are just one of the perks of writing spicy books.

"How do you know he does non-fiction?"

"When I was on the plane and looking up Julian, his name came up." I open my audiobook app and search for his name. I click on one of the samples and turn up the volume. We listen to a description of the castles in Scotland for a minute. There's something familiar about his voice, but I can't place it. I'm sure I've heard it before.

"Maybe I'll come by your booth and see if he's as sexy as he sounds," Amanda chuckles.

"Scotland castles do it for you?" I eye her with suspicion.

"Why not? But he's probably rocking a dad-bod and is a decade older than me."

I bark out a laugh. "Girl, what are you talking about? That's your type!"

"Hey now, that's not my *only* type. Give me a sexy younger man with an accent and I'll have him on my knees, worshiping the ground I walk on. Sometimes my FemDom energy needs to come out. Don't wait up for me on Saturday…"

# 8

# BECCA

In a rideshare packed full of my promo materials, I'm headed to one of my favorite conventions of the year, stuck in typical NYC traffic. Amanda got there thirty minutes ago and is scoping out the place.

"How's it looking?"

Amanda switches to video call. "See for yourself." She pans the phone to reveal a room full of half-prepared tables and boxes, everyone working to set up their displays. I nod and Amanda switches back to selfie mode. "Did you bring your promos?"

"*Did I bring my promos?*" I roll my eyes. "Is this my first rodeo?"

"No, I meant the extra spicy ones that we have to block out on social media." She bites her lip.

"Yeah, why?"

"Oh, no reason. Okay, I have to set up my table. I'll see you in a bit."

We hang up and, twenty minutes later, my ride pulls up to the convention center. I text Amanda to let her know I arrived and head inside to get checked in.

Once I have my badge, I find my table, hoping and praying to all of the deities that my books arrived. I've heard my fair share of horror stories of authors' books arriving late or not at all, so every convention I'm nervous that this is the time mine won't show. Thankfully, when I reach my table, I find several boxes of books waiting for me.

While pulling books out of the boxes, I quickly glance over at the table next to me. The mystery narrator has no headshots and his table is void of any personality. His voice might be sexy as fuck, but I'm convinced this guy will end up being a sweet, seventy-year-old man. I chuckle at the thought.

Grabbing the last of the books and setting them on the table, someone's hand splays across my stomach and pulls me back against their hard chest.

*Shit, is this how I die? At a book convention? I suppose there are worse ways to go.*

"Hello, my Becca," the voice purrs beside my ear, making the hair on my neck stand up.

*Am I living in a real life stalker romance? And to think I used to give the heroines crap for not running.*

I spin around and... *Julian?*

"Crap, you scared me. What are you doing here? I thought it was sold out for authors and narrators."

Julian leans in, his breath tickling my ear as he replies, "I'm here to see the infamous Merlot Bennet." He kisses my cheek and chuckles as he pulls back. "I applied after we spoke about it and they emailed me to confirm a spot was open."

"You have a table? I didn't see your name on the list." I wouldn't have missed it. Before every event, I meticulously study the attending author and narrator lists for networking.

He gestures to the table next to us. "Kincade."

"That's…" It clicks. "You narrate under two names."

"Ah, she's as smart as she is beautiful."

I smirk. "If that's the case, I must be a bridge troll."

Frowning, he insists, "There's no way you could have known. I use a different voice for my nonfiction work and make sure my face isn't used in any promotions… and you are the furthest thing from a bridge troll."

I'm about to contradict him when I spot Layla approaching from the corner of my eye. "You'll have to excuse me." I step away from Julian and practically run into Layla's arms. "Book bestie! How the fuck have you been?"

She squeezes me tighter. "Fucking fantastic." She then whispers, "Who is that hot guy you were talking to? Single? Gay? I need all the details."

I resist looking behind me, instead linking my arm with hers and walking in the opposite direction. "That's Julian Evans. He's narrating *Delivery of Fate*."

"Doesn't he do fantasy? I thought you were using John for it."

"Yeah, that's a whole other story that will need margaritas and all you can eat tacos." I check the time on my phone with a dramatic sigh. "Not sure we could get either at 7am. How about a coffee instead?"

We head toward the coffee cart and, when I glance back, Julian's eyes are still on us.

---

Amanda, Layla, and I finish setting up our tables just in time for doors to open at 10am. I brought my steamiest promo materials, thinking my table buddy was some stuffy nonfiction guy. I'm incredibly embarrassed now that I know it's Julian. He knows what I write, but it doesn't make it any less awkward.

Stephanie, my assistant, isn't here yet, so I send her a quick text.

> Hey there. Just checking in. Do you have an ETA?

I stuff my phone back in my pocket as a few readers approach my table for personalized signed paperbacks. After about fifteen minutes of back-to-back conversations with excited readers, I check my phone to find a voicemail from Stephanie saying she has a high fever and can't keep anything down.

*Shit.*

I hate working events on my own, especially ones this big. I won't have a chance to visit with other authors until after the signing expo ends.

"Everything okay?" Julian asks.

"Yeah, it'll be fine." I nod, drawing in a shaky breath. In the time it took me to listen to the voicemail, no less than thirty readers lined up to meet me. I glance back to Julian who's grinning and biting his lip.

"It'll be great," he insists.

Today is going to be a nightmare.

---

For three straight hours, I sign books and chat with some of the most amazing readers I've met to date. It has been a fantasy, not a nightmare. I feel a little bad that almost no one has visited the table next to me, but Julian has been nowhere to be found for the last few hours. Readers don't want to talk to an assistant, no matter how friendly Julian's assistant seems to be.

Layla appears next to my table and offers, "All right, girly. I'll hold your line so you can have a bathroom break,"

There's still a line of twenty or so, waiting patiently. I make a quick announcement. "Sorry everyone! I need to take ten. Potty break, you know how it is." My readers are so incredibly gracious and not a single one of them groan or even leave the line. "Thank you, Layla," I whisper to her.

I rush to the bathroom, anxious to get back to my table. After a quick bathroom break, I'm jogging back when I spot Julian talking with a few romance authors. I slow my pace and my nosey self can't help but notice that they're laughing with his hand on the small of one of their backs. I do a double take. Yep, his hand is an inch from her ass as he presses a kiss to her cheek.

*He's a touchy person who flirts with everyone… I'm not special.*

No wonder I was so attracted to him. This feels like Bryan 2.0; he sucked me in with his charisma and promises, only to have his hands on the next available pussy he could find. I'm drawn toward men who are bigger red flags than even a matador could handle.

I'm disgusted and embarrassed that I entertained the idea of sleeping with him on more than one occasion. He doesn't even narrate romance, but is surrounded by authors who *only* write love stories. How did I not see this before? He's only flirting with me because I'm a top 10 author. He isn't narrating my book because he likes me, he's doing it to further his career.

It's risky to consider any sort of relationship with Julian. The contract has a non-fraternization policy—one I insisted on for all my contracts, after everything happened with Bryan. This is the wake up call I needed.

I rush back to my table and Layla's eyebrows shoot up in surprise when she spots me. I must be wearing all of my emotions on my face. I shake my head to signal that I am in no mood to talk about it. She nods in solidarity and, when I reach her, she asks, "When do we start the tequila shots?"

One of the readers overhears and chimes in. "The bar just opened. Can we grab you a drink?"

Layla's lips turn up in a smirk. "Give me five minutes. Who wants to do shots with the amazing Merlot Bennet?"

My shes, gays, and theys in line squeal with excitement. This is either going to be the best or worst idea Layla has ever come up with.

# JULIAN

I've spent the last few hours networking and haven't seen Becca anywhere. I assumed she would be out here shaking hands like I am, but other than right when the convention opened, she's nowhere to be found. She had a bit of a line when I left my table earlier, so there's a chance it never died down.

I make my way back to my table where my assistant is holding down the fort. I take over, giving her a much needed and deserved break. I'm sure she's bored out of her mind, since no one is here to see me.

While out networking, I ran into one of my best friends from college, who's starting out as an indie author. Ingrid is so talented; I'm sure she'll do amazing things if she's mentored under the wing of other romance authors. If Becca is up to it, I'd love to introduce them.

As I approach my table, there's hysterical laughter coming from Becca's. A crowd of at least fifty readers surrounds her. I circle behind my table to get a better view, since the crowd is now encroaching on my space.

Sitting on top of her table with her legs crossed, Becca lifts her glass of wine and clinks it with the couple in front of her. "Congratulations! When is the big day?"

One of the women replies, "Not until August." They look at each other. "Would you want to come?"

"Fuck yes, I would," Becca cheers, pulling out her phone. "What's your social media handle? I'll add you. Message me when invitations go out and I'll be there! If I can't, I'll send you all the sapphic merch and character art I can commission so you can make that dickhead dad of yours super uncomfortable."

They all laugh and I can't help but join in. Becca exudes so much joy and light, it's infectious. I come up behind her and whisper in her ear. "Up for taking a walk with me?"

She startles and nearly falls off the table, spilling wine in her lap. "Fucking hell, Julian. You can't keep sneaking up behind me like that." One of the men waiting in line takes out a shirt from his bag and hands it to her to clean up. "Thanks, guys. Aw, damn it! These were my favorite pants, too. Red wine does *not* come out of linen."

"Sorry, Becca, I didn't mean—" She glares at me and I quickly realize my slip up. I clear my throat. "I mean, should I get a fresh bottle of merlot for Merlot?" *Good save.*

"It's the least you can do," another woman says, eyeing me up and down like I'm milk that's turned.

"I'm sorry, Becca," I whisper, kissing her cheek. She doesn't hum like she normally does when I touch her.

*Something's wrong.*

I head to the bar to grab wine and glasses. I also find a replacement shirt for the guy who was faster than I was to help clean up the mess.

Walking back, the author at the booth across from Becca's is giving me the side eye. Who knew spilt wine could turn so many people against me? I walk behind her table, set everything down, and pour a fresh glass for Becca.

"Here you go." I hand her a glass and cheers erupt from the crowd that grew exponentially since I left.

She ignores me and continues with a story, "So, as I was saying, DVP is totally possible in real life. I'd show you, but I want to get invited back here next year." The crowd laughs and she finally looks at me. "Did you need something, Julian?" Her tone is ice cold. At least on the plane when she gave me short answers, it was playful. This is worse than a brush-off.

The author from the booth across from ours comes over and interrupts the festivities. "All right everyone. Everything is closing up for the panels. We can't get Merlot any more drunk than she already is, or she'll be napping on stage." There are groans, so the woman adds, "She'll be signing copies for anyone who is in line." Excited whispers fill the space and everyone lines up.

"I'm Layla, by the way, and you're in my spot."

"Oh, sorry." I move out of her way.

"All right, I'll be your assistant. What do you need, Ms. Bennet?"

Becca laughs and, as she's about to reply, her friend Amanda approaches. "Who got drunk and forgot to invite me?" Amanda and Layla prep stickers and bookmarks in all of the books to help Becca keep the line moving.

*Where is her assistant? They should be fired for leaving her like this.*

I'm not sure what's going on with Becca, but I can tell she doesn't want me here. I grab my bag and leave with my assistant to find a good seat for the panel she's on. At least then I'll be able to see her in her glory and not giving me a death stare.

―――――

Ingrid takes a seat to my left as the moderator begins. Her girlfriend, Trinity, is also on the panel; she's a fellow narrator who specializes in erotica. "Welcome everyone. We have a variety of authors and narrators to discuss today's topic: Spicy Audiobooks."

*Maybe next year I'll be asked to join?*

I rest my arm on the back of Ingrid's chair and whisper, "Isn't she stunning? Fuck, I'm out of my league." Ingrid laughs, but it's cut short to listen to one of the panelists answer the first question that I missed because I couldn't keep my eyes off Becca.

"I prefer duet narration when doing books with on-page explicit scenes. When I did *Begging for the Billionaire*, it was helpful having Brenda doing the part of Jennifer in the book. It's not impossible for a male narrator to do non-male characters, but when you add in the steamier scenes, it hits differently, you know?" I actually agree with him, even if my experience with romance is limited. I've narrated scenes in fantasy books, but nothing close to what Becca writes.

Wait... *Begging for the Billionaire*? He narrated for Becca?

"Thank you, Bryan." The audience claps and the moderator continues, "I'm sure working with your wife is helpful when you're looking for chemistry in an audio-book. Trinity, would you mind answering the same question, since you specialize in sapphic books with duet narration?"

*Bryan... Brenda... Oh. Fuck.*

I can't pay attention to Trinity's answer; my eyes are locked on Becca. Her jaw ticks as she writes something on the paper in front of her. I've only known her a week, but it doesn't take a genius to figure out that she's trying her best to keep it together. I swear there are fumes coming out of her ears. This is so incredibly fucked up.

"Thank you, Trinity. Next, we'd love to hear from Merlot. You worked with Bryan on two of your other books, but there wasn't an audiobook for *Delivery of Fate* until now. Can you explain the process of looking for a new narrator?" The moderator passes the microphone to Becca.

"Yes, Bryan narrated my debut novel. When *Begging for the Billionaire* took off, I moved from indie to traditional publishing. My publisher liked the audiobook that we produced together, so they insisted that he do *Billionaire* as well with… Brenda." Becca pauses and takes a sip of water, likely to calm whatever emotions she's feeling. "When my publisher picked up *Delivery of Fate* and repackaged it for rerelease, I needed a different voice for it." Becca's eyes meet mine. "We stumbled upon Julian Evans and he's perfect for the part."

"You know, Merlot, Brenda and I could do *Delivery of Fate*… if you change your mind," Bryan suggests with a smirk that I want to wipe off with my fist.

*Asshole.*

My hand flexes, then balls at my side. Ingrid whispers, "Not worth it, buddy. This guy is a total douche, but he's not taking your contract. Everyone knows the two of them dated and he left Merlot for the other narrator. She would never cast him over you. I think *Delivery of Fate* is actually a break-up retelling."

My attention is pulled back to Becca. "I needed someone who gives growly, high fae energy, so a fantasy narrator is the perfect choice." Becca glances at me briefly and returns her attention to Bryan. "So, I think I'm all set."

"See, told you." Ingrid nudges me with her elbow.

"Why would they be on a panel together?" My jaw ticks and I have an unexplainable urge to protect Becca, even if she can hold her own.

"John backed out at the last minute. Family emergency. I offered, but they wanted a male narrator who did romance for the discussions," Ingrid explains.

This has to be why Becca was so short with me earlier. Who the hell wants to do a panel with their ex? I had no idea she had to work with him after the cheating. I shake my head in disbelief and lean in to whisper, "I think I'm fucked."

Ingrid frowns. "Why? I told you, he's not going to take it from you."

"No, not that. I fucking like her… *a lot*. But I don't think I have a chance with her." I rake my hand through my hair.

"I'm not into men, but I'll admit, you're a catch. Go for it. A piece of advice, though, you might want to look single while you try to woo the biggest name in the romance industry." She removes my arm from behind her chair and nods toward the stage. Becca's eyes dart away as soon as I look her direction.

*Damn it!* On top of everything else, it probably looks like I'm flirting with Ingrid.

For the next half hour, I'm not paying attention to anything but Becca. At one point, Layla hands Becca a shot of what looks like tequila and the crowd goes nuts. There were whispers behind me about how much they love Merlot and that they'll be rushing to her table as soon as this is over to grab all of her books. I sink further into my chair. Trying to get Becca's attention today is going to be a challenge.

The panel comes to a close and the moderator thanks everyone for their time. I kiss Ingrid on the cheek and whisper, "I'll catch you later. I need to see about a girl."

# 10

## BECCA

What started out as one of my favorite conventions has taken a turn for the worse. Not only was I forced to do a panel with my ex, I had to watch a guy I thought I liked flirt with a beautiful woman in the crowd. I risk the jinx and mutter to myself, "Could today get any worse?"

As I make it back to my table, there's forty or fifty readers lined up. I internally swear; I'm going to run out of books.

Amanda and Layla are waiting for me. "You guys don't need to stick around. Get back to your tables, you have your own readers to meet!" I insist.

"Um, have you seen the line? It's all the way outside. They aren't here for us, they're here for you. Plus, our assistants can send our readers over to your table and we can sign here," Amanda says with a shrug. "We're in this together ladies. Fuck that Evans guy and fuck Bryan."

Layla pours three shots of tequila. Mixing wine and tequila isn't the best idea, but Amanda, being the mom of our little group, has trash bags ready. I hope we won't need them.

"To the amazingly talented Merlot Bennet!" Layla raises her glass and the crowd booms with cheers.

Despite how I'm feeling, my heart soars at the sound. Maybe it was an anti-jinx. This is too fucking cool.

We down our shots without chasers, which earns us more applause. "Thank you for helping me. I don't know what I would do without you two." I wrap my arms around them. "Okay, let's do this."

Amanda preps the books with smutty stickers and bookmarks, and Layla handles my book sales. I'm able to focus my attention on my amazing readers.

A couple approaches and they are far too attractive for words. I take note of their appearance for a later date. She has dark auburn hair, piercing sky blue eyes, and is in great shape for a woman who might be in her forties. The man is around the same age, with sandy blond hair, tattoos on both forearms peeking through a button up shirt expertly cuffed. I like the contrast between the ink and the dress shirt. "That was amazing," the woman squeals. "Fuck that narrator. I heard about how that all went down with you two. My authors refuse to work with him and Brenda because of it."

"Em, you can't be word-vomiting on her. It's *the* Merlot Bennet, for Loki's sake." He hands me a book to sign. "You were incredible, Merlot. That man is ketchup pre-cum; not worth your time. *Vacation with the Enemy* is one of my all time favorites, by the way."

I chuckle. "Thanks. Who should I make this out to?"

He picks up three more copies of *Vacation with the Enemy*. "One for Sage, Mel, Charlotte and one made out to the magnificent Ethan Barlowe." The woman sets one more copy on the stack. "And, apparently, one for Emma."

"You wouldn't, by chance, need representation?" Emma asks. "That was quite the panel, and I'd love to work with you."

"I'm happy with Cassie, but thank you." It's always awkward talking to agents and publishers. I'm still pretty new to traditional publishing and miss the days when I could just write, send off to an editor, and put it out into the universe whenever I felt like it.

"If you change your mind, I'll be the first in line." She hands me her card. *Emma Alexander.*

"All right, enough sales pitching, Em." Ethan smacks her arm.

I finish signing their books, and he asks, "Up for another shot? Name your price. It would be the highlight of my life. Just don't tell my wife I said that. Or my kids…"

Emma laughs. "I'm totally telling Mel." I assumed these two were married, but it appears they're just good friends. "Thanks again, Merlot. You're amazing."

Layla pours five shots. "All right, let's do this."

The five of us take our shots and I decide this has to be the last one I do for a while—I want to be buzzed, not drunk. "Thanks for coming today. It was great meeting you two." Emma and Ethan walk away and the line has only grown.

About to greet the reader approaching, Julian's familiar purr comes from behind, startling me. "You might need these." He sets down a bottle of water and an individually packaged aspirin. I don't turn or acknowledge him.

Amanda gives him a side eye. "My girl can handle her liquor."

I chuckle softly. "Amanda, it's fine."

"I'm sorry, I'll go. Let me know if you need anything." Julian's footsteps echo on the cement floor as he walks away.

There might not be anything romantic between us, but we'll be working together, so I should at least thank him for the friendly gesture. He's just trying to be nice.

"Julian." He turns. "Thank you." Our eyes lock and it's as if time stops. There's a hunger in his gaze and I can count on one hand how many times someone has looked at me like this. All of those times were him. I can't look away.

Layla's throat clears, pulling me from whatever the hell that was. I return my attention to the readers. "Hi there. Who should I make this out to?"

---

The last few hours were a blur. Amanda and Layla were amazing and I don't think I ever would've been able to get through the line without them. Their assistants brought over boxes of their books and all of us sold out before the convention was even over.

Layla insists there's an amazing Mexican food restaurant a block away, so we grab a few bottles of water and chug them before heading out. We need to sober up before the VIP reader event tonight.

Four carne asada tacos and a heaping serving of guacamole and chips later, I'm definitely on my way to being presentable in a professional setting. This convention is the only one I've been to that served alcohol, and while it makes it a fun experience, I need to be more careful next time.

Seeing Bryan today should have had more of an effect on me, but I was too caught up in how it felt to see Julian with the other authors. *Man, I know how to pick 'em.*

"So, what's going on with Julian? And why was he hotter today than when we saw him at the hotel bar?" Amanda asks, placing her credit card in the leather folder.

I was really hoping to avoid the whole Julian discussion. I sigh. "There's nothing going on with him. He's a big flirt, and he's probably just using me to break into the romance genre."

"Sucks you have to work with him, I would have tapped that already. I saw the way he looked at you. Guy is crushing hard," Amanda insists.

"He was flirting with a woman during the panel. I'm telling you: he's just a flirt. He's not into me like that." *Even if we did kiss. It must have meant nothing to him.*

Amanda laughs. "You mean Ingrid? She's with Trinity. If he was flirting with her, he's barking up the wrong tree."

"He was a little touchy-feely with a few other authors, though." Layla shrugs. "I doubt he's using you, but he definitely wants to get in your pants."

"Speaking of assholes who use people." Amanda gestures to the door. Bryan and Brenda walk in.

*Fuck.* I can't even enjoy guacamole in peace.

They approach our table. "Well, isn't this a pleasant surprise," Brenda says, a little too sickeningly sweet. "Can we join you?"

"We were just leaving." I stand. "Excuse me. I'm going to use the restroom before heading back."

I walk quickly to the bathroom that I don't need to use. I'll wait it out until our bill is settled up.

Ten minutes of pacing later, I get a text from Layla that we're ready to go but that Julian is here, too. I wash my hands, reapply my blue-red lipstick, and walk out. I need to get out of here, fast. I take the corner too quickly and face-plant into a hard chest.

"Slow down, kitten."

I suck in a breath and my stomach drops. *Bryan.* "Sorry, I didn't see you there."

Bryan's fingers trace up my arm. A few years ago, the sensation would have lit me up inside. Now, it makes me so incredibly disgusted that I resist the urge to rush back in the bathroom and throw up my delicious tacos and guac.

"I've missed you. You know, Brenda and I have an open marriage..."

"Don't touch me," I grit out, swatting his hand away.

"Oh, I miss your feistiness."

He tries to touch me again but I step back. I glance behind me. *Shit. There's nowhere to go.* "I need to get back to Layla and Amanda."

Bryan grabs my wrist to stop me as I attempt to move past him. Thankfully, the men's room opens and I look to the approaching stranger with a plea in my eyes. As if my hallway experience couldn't get any more fucked up, the man who walks out is none other than Julian.

*Of course.*

Julian's eyes shoot daggers at Bryan as he clenches his jaw. "You heard her. Get your hands off Becca, before I remove them for you."

"This doesn't concern you," Bryan spits.

Julian smirks. "You're touching my girl. How does that not concern me?"

*His girl? What the fuck?*

Bryan releases my wrist and leans in to whisper. "You know you'll always be mine, kitten." His words have bile rising in my throat.

Julian takes my hand without a word and walks me through the restaurant, stopping at the bar to pick up a to-go order. He then leads me outside, where my friends are waiting.

He breaks the silence. "Are you okay?"

I look down at our joined hands. "Um…" Neither one of us lets go. *I should let go, right?*

"Come on, let's get back." Amanda's voice pulls me from whatever spell Julian has me under.

"Right," I agree. "We should go."

The four of us make our way down the street. Julian slows our pace and whispers. "Sorry about all that. Figured you could use a short lived fake dating trope."

"That I did," I hum.

"Wouldn't mind if it wasn't fake, though."

# 11

# JULIAN

Becca stops walking and lets go of my hand. "Hey guys, go ahead. I'll catch up," she says to her friends.

Amanda and Layla glance back at us with worry but Becca gives them a look that apparently satisfies them. They continue on their way back to the convention center.

"Everything okay?" I ask cautiously. "We should get back." There's a short rumble of thunder and we both look up. "There's a good chance we'll get caught in the rain if we don't move quickly."

"What the fuck is this, Julian? I know you're not interested in me. So, please stop with the flirting."

I feel like I've been slapped with her words. "What on earth gave you the impression that I'm not interested in you?"

"I don't know what your game is. Are you trying to break into the romance genre for audiobooks? Or do you just hit on every woman you come across?" She chews on her lip. "Nevermind, I don't want the answer to that. Just… please stop making me feel things. It sucks."

I swear internally; Ingrid was right, Becca thinks I'm some kind of player. I take a step toward her. "First of all, I don't want to narrate romance books. I'm perfectly content doing high fantasy and nonfiction. I'm only doing your book because I wanted an excuse to spend time with you. Second, I know we don't know each other very well, but do you think I just go around kissing women I find incredibly attractive?" I close the distance. "You think you're the only one who doesn't understand this? You need to stop making *me* feel things. I haven't been able to think of anything else but you since we met. That's not normal."

"You don't…" She looks away as her voice trails off.

"I don't *what?* Like you? Fuck. How much more clear do I need to be?" I slide my hand into her hair and bring her delicious red lips to mine. I can't help myself. This woman has had me under her spell since the moment we met, and I'll be damned if I let her slip out of my grasp. I drop my to-go bag and pull her impossibly closer. She doesn't push away, sighing into my embrace. "Yeah, I fucking like you, my Becca… *just* you," I mutter against her lips.

The clouds open up, a light mist dusts both of us. She pulls back. "We shouldn't be doing this."

"I'm not asking you to fall in love with me." I look to the sky. The mist is quickly turning into heavy droplets. I return my gaze to her—this beautiful goddess of a woman who has enchanted me. "Are you up for a bookworthy moment?"

She chuckles with a furrowed brow. "What are you talking about?"

"Come on." I take her hand and lead her away from the busy sidewalk, a few steps down one of the narrow alleys. "When was the last time you were properly kissed in the rain?" I guide her backwards, up against one of the brick buildings. "When, Becca?" I ask softly.

Her eyes cast downward and she shakes her head. "Never."

I tilt her chin up so she'll look at me and slide half of my hand to cup her neck, my thumb brushing her cheek. "Feel free to include this in your next book, then." I kiss her again, this time unrushed and savoring each time my tongue glides over hers. Her body melts into mine, fitting perfectly against me like a missing piece of a puzzle. I don't know how I'll ever kiss another woman after her.

When we finally break apart, our breath in sync and heavy, she whispers, "Time stops, they feel a zing course through their bodies, the air crackles between them, and… their breath hitches."

I can't help but chuckle at her echo of our conversation on the plane. "See, I knew you felt it too. What are you doing to me, my Becca?"

"*Your* Becca?"

"Yeah. *My* Becca. I'm supposed to be in California, basking in the sunshine. Instead, I'm here, kissing a beautiful woman in the rain. A woman I met a week ago has me worshiping at her altar. You're the writer; I'm sure you could come up with a thousand better ways I could refer to you."

Becca's breath catches at the word 'writer,' and her eyes dart between mine. "Julian, we can't do this. You know it's in the contract. If we get caught..." She shakes her head. "I agree there's something happening between us that I can't explain but this can't happen."

"If I wasn't under contract, would things be different?" I ask hopefully.

"I don't know, maybe."

"Then, I'll walk away from your book."

She chuckles softly. "You know I was hoping for a different voice than John's. Yours is perfect. I need you... your voice, I mean. So, this"—she gestures between us—"has to end, no matter how much I don't want it to. I need to get back. The VIP reader party starts soon and I'm a bit of a mess." I brush a few wet strands off her forehead and a small smirk tugs at her lips. "For the record, that will most definitely be going in one of my books."

I take her chin between my thumb and forefinger and pull her mouth back to mine. She whimpers against my lips and allows me to tease her until she opens for me. Her arms wrap around my neck and I fight the urge to take things further. "What if no one knows?" I ask between kisses. "What if behind closed doors, it's just you and me? I can't bear the thought of not kissing you again."

She moans into my mouth and I'm a fucking goner. I pull her leg up and over my hip, pressing my now incredibly hard cock against her center. My hand slides down her leg, gripping her thigh. There is nothing innocent about how I'm touching her. As if reading my thoughts, she pulls back and touches her swollen lips.

"Can I have one night? Clothes on or off, I don't care. Give me one night."

Becca clucks her tongue. "One night? Then, you'll still do my book and won't press for more?"

"You have my word."

## 12

---

# BECCA

*Do I want him to press for more?*

*Why the hell am I so into this guy I met a week ago?*

*If anyone finds out…*

"So, is that a yes?" Julian's words pull me from my thoughts.

"I, uh, need to get to the party." I move past him, out of the alleyway and onto the main sidewalk. Julian chases after me; I expected nothing less.

"Becca, I'm sorry if I overstepped…"

I spin to face him and can't hide my amusement. "I didn't say no, did I?"

"I can take you out tonight?"

"Maybe." I shrug and turn back toward the convention center. I don't make it two steps before he takes my hand. While I don't mind indulging him in this flirtatious game we have going on, I need to be careful. We're under contract, so no one can know what happens tonight if I go out with him. I pull my hand back. "Not here. I can't risk being seen with you this way. It would end badly for both of us."

We approach the stoplight and I watch the pedestrian light intently, praying the little walking man lights up quickly so we can cross. "You expect me to go a few hours without being near you? Without touching you?" He rests his hand on my lower back and leans in to whisper, "The minute the event is over, you're mine for the rest of the night."

My breath hitches. *Man, he has a way with words. Of course he does, he's a damn audiobook narrator.* I straighten my posture, focusing my attention on the lit up red hand that has me rooted in place. I write smut for a living but this man, with his sexy as fuck voice and his book boyfriend energy, is doing things for me that no book ever has.

Thunder booms overhead before another sheet of rain is dumped on us. "Come on. Let's get you dried off." Julian pulls me to the side, right as the light finally turned green for us to cross. He hails a cab and, thankfully, one pulls up almost instantly. We get in and he looks at me. "What's your address?"

"Oh, no. We aren't going back to my place. Absolutely not. Nice try, though." I narrow my eyes.

He chuckles and gives his hotel information to the driver. It's only a few minutes from here but there's still the issue of my soaked clothes and the VIP reader party starting soon. As if reading my mind, he offers, "There's a shop next door to my hotel; we can stop and get you fresh clothes."

I look down, laughing to myself. "Yeah, I'm pretty sure these aren't presentable for a meet and greet party with readers."

"They love you; I'm sure they wouldn't care either way. But, we can't have you uncomfortable now, can we? Especially since you have plans after," he says with a wink.

Julian's hand is in mine again and he lets out a contented sigh. I get a flashback to the first time on the plane. He said he just got out of a serious relationship, so it could explain his being so affectionate—force of habit. Someone hurt this man and, if I ever meet them, I'll either destroy them or thank them. Maybe both.

I feel comfortable with him, like we've known each other for years. In this whirlwind of a week, I've felt an unexplainable pull to him—unlike anything I've ever experienced. Being with him would be a risk. Is it a risk I'm willing to take?

*Yes.*

Right now, the only one who could ever tell on us is the cabbie, so I do the one reckless and impulsive thing I've wanted to do since I stepped away from him in the alley... I kiss him.

---

"Blue or green?" I ask, holding up two different dresses.

"Black." Julian ignores my suggestions and pulls a dress off the rack that's not only incredibly expensive but also entirely too revealing. Granted, it's a reader event where most of them consume a spicy book a day and wouldn't be phased by my showing up looking a little like a high-end lady of the night. While it has a high neckline, it's backless and will land just above my ass. "Try it on."

It's in my size; he's been paying attention.

I take the dress from him, along with the blue and green ones, and find a fitting room. The blue one is stunning but the color doesn't do me any favors. The green doesn't fit properly. In true Goldilocks fashion, the black one is just right. It hugs my curves perfectly, and while it's not something I would pick out for myself, it's perfect for the event. Now, my only concern is what to wear on this date I haven't technically agreed to yet.

I step out of the fitting rooms and do a little twirl. "Well, you were right."

"*Fuck.*" Julian's gaze roams my body, his eyes as dark and ravenous as if I walked out here naked.

"Hypothetically speaking, if I were to join you later this evening, would this be appropriate to wear?" I look down at the dress and back to him. Our eyes lock and, for several moments, neither one of us blinks. I can't explain this gravitational pull I have toward him.

*Static electricity. Time stops. Air Crackles. Breaths hitch.*

My feet have a mind of their own and I take a few steps toward him. "Will this work?" I ask softly. Two more steps and I close the distance, leaving only inches between us.

Julian gulps, pulling my attention to his mouth. "You decide the attire and I'll take care of the rest."

"*If* I say yes."

A smirk tugs at his lips. "You will."

"So confident." I realize I've been staring at his lips for far too long and, when our eyes meet again, I lose myself in the flecks of gold in his light brown eyes.

He reaches for the tag on my shoulder and carefully opens the safety pin holding it in place, removing it. "Ready to go?"

"Sure, I just need to pay for this over-the-top dress." I attempt a step back but he wraps his arm around me, splaying his hand on my very naked back and pulling me to him.

Before I can say anything, he lifts a receipt from his pocket, brandishing it between his middle and forefinger. "I beat you to it, *my Becca*."

I snatch it out of his hand and check to see if he actually spent $12,000 on the dress. Spoiler: he did.

"I can't accept this." He releases his hold on me but his fingers trace up my spine, lighting me on fire. "It's too much." My words come out strangled. "How... how did you know it would even fit? How can you *afford* it? Sorry, that was rude, but you're a *fantasy narrator*. Not exactly the most lucrative profession to be tossing around $12,000 on a dress."

*How much money does this guy have?* I know he owns a winery; I just assumed it was inherited or something. He seems so down-to-earth; not a guy who buys Valentino on a whim.

"Are you ready to head out?"

"Answer the question, Julian."

He chuckles. "Agree to go out with me tonight and I'll tell you."

"Fine. Yes, I'll go tonight." I eye him suspiciously. "Now, out with it."

Julian leans in. His hot breath on my neck causes my heart to race. "I'll tell you tonight." He presses a warm kiss to my neck before straightening. "Come on. You still need to get ready for the party."

---

*Get it together, Becca! He's just a guy. A hot guy. But still... just a guy! Keep it in your pants.*

I blow dry my hair and reapply my lipstick. Thankfully, my mascara is waterproof and survived the rain. I'm severely overdressed, so I need to keep my makeup understated.

Walking out of the bathroom, I find Julian working at his computer with his headphones on. When he spots me, he pulls them off his ears and rests them around his neck.

"Well, don't you clean up nice?" I tease. He's wearing an

expensive tux, which causes yet another alarm bell to go off in my head.

*How is he able to afford this suite, this dress, first class, his tux…?*

"If I'm going to be your date tonight, I need to look the part," he says with a shrug.

"Hold on there. You said *after* the party. You can't go as my date *to* the party."

Julian removes the headphones from his neck and stands. "I can go as your date, under the guise of being your new narrator for the book." He circles the table. "We'll tell them we're friends."

"We aren't friends." I take a step toward him. "I don't think you ever wanted to be my friend, Julian. But if I'm being honest, I never wanted to be your friend, either." He stays rooted in place and I take another step, slower this time. "Friends don't ask you what you name your pussy."

He bites his lip. "I don't suppose they do. I'm still waiting on that answer, my Becca."

*There he goes with the "my Becca" again…*

"I'll never tell." I raise my chin.

"I don't believe you've ever given me a straight answer to any of my questions. At the risk of another non-answer, I still have to ask, what is it that you want?"

I look away. "It's not that simple." *Damn it, I've seen The Notebook too many times…* He closes the distance but I refuse to meet his gaze. "I don't have the luxury of getting what I want."

He gently tilts my chin with his thumb and forefinger, forcing me to look at him. There it is again—that spark that only happens in books. "What do you want?" he asks again.

"Right now?" Our chests flush, breath in sync, and a moment stretches between us before I quietly admit, "You."

# 13

## JULIAN

Becca's eyes dart between mine. I've never had a woman look at me the way she is right now. I lied when I said I would be okay with just tonight. There's no way in hell I'm going to let her go after... whatever this is.

Neither of us say a word.

Whatever response I might have had is cut off by my phone buzzing on the coffee table. It startles both of us and draws her attention from me. *Whoever it is, they're dead to me.* Becca just admitted she wants me, I'm not letting this moment go so easily.

I cup her cheek and her gaze returns to me. A smirk tugs at my lips. "I'm going to kiss you now, and—"

Taking me by surprise, she grabs the lapels of my jacket and pulls me closer until our faces are less than an inch apart. Holding me there, she pauses for only a moment.

"You're going to let me," Becca finishes my sentence and kisses me roughly.

I slide my hand into her hair to guide her where I want her. She may have made the first move but she lets me take control almost immediately. It's raw, feverish, and all of this feels... right. My skin is on fire; I can't get close enough to her. I strip off my tux jacket and toss it to the floor, returning my hands to each side of her face as I kiss the ever loving hell out of her.

She reaches for my belt and, as much as I'd love to sink myself inside her right now, I want to take my time. We have to leave in a few minutes; it's not nearly enough time for me to worship every inch of her like I've been fantasizing about all week.

I grip her wrist, stopping her. "Later. If I only get tonight, as you requested, then I want you spread out on that bed while I feast on your... *lady garden* for hours before I fuck you so hard you can't walk for a month."

She throws her head back and lets out the most adorable laugh I've ever heard. It's music to my ears. "You're a fucking tease. Maybe I was right about you and you're just a big flirt," she says with a seductive smile. "You have me in your hotel room, wearing a scrap of fabric for a dress, and we're *not* going to have sex?"

I tangle my hand in her hair and tug with just enough force that her giggles are cut short. I kiss her neck and whisper, "You're mine for the night, my Becca. If I say you have to wait, you're gonna be a good fucking girl and wait." Goosebumps erupt down her arms and a soft whimper escapes her. I'm going to have far too much fun teasing her tonight. No matter how much I want to touch her, we need to leave. I release her and grab my jacket and toss it over my shoulder, holding it with my hooked middle and forefinger. "Ready?" I ask, offering my arm.

If I have any say in it, she'll be mine for more than tonight.

———

The VIP tickets were sold out. I'm not a big-time narrator, so I wasn't asked to attend in a professional capacity. But, a generous donation to the convention organizers guaranteed me entry. As much as I feel a pull to be near Becca, I decide that keeping my distance is a safer option and will give me the opportunity to rile her up a bit. She's like a lioness in a cage right now—a little taunting will have her pouncing on me later.

I find a quiet spot away from her adoring fans but her eyes still find me through the crowd. Even from across the room, I see the blush on her cheeks. She turns away first, when a reader approaches her.

I can't help but admire her from afar for a good fifteen minutes. The way she carries herself, how she gives each and every one of the readers her undivided attention, *her delicious body that beacons me to touch her…*

Fuck this. I can't sit here and not be near her. I make my way through the hoard of readers until I reach my siren. I place my hand on the small of her back, relishing the feel of her naked skin against my palm. I lean in to whisper, "Sorry, I really did try to stay away."

Becca's cheeks flush and she clears her throat. "Have you all met Julian Evans? He's my new narrator for *Delivery of Fate*."

They all look at me. There's a chorus of murmurs and whispers. One asks, "Could you read something for us?"

I raise my empty hand. "I didn't prepare anything and, unfortunately, I can't do a scene from *Delivery of Fate* since it's still in production," I reply.

"How about *Vacation with the Enemy*?" a man asks. He hands me his copy. I open it to find it's already signed by Becca, addressed to *The Magnificent Ethan Barlowe*. I chuckle and continue to flip through the dedication, content warnings, playlist, and table of contents, until I finally reach the prologue.

"Is this okay, Merlot?" I look at her before I begin to make sure she's comfortable. Becca nods and I clear my throat. "*Three weeks. I have three weeks to make Daphne see that I'm not who she thinks I am. Three weeks to win over the woman I've obsessed over for years. Three weeks to make her mine. There's a fine line between hate and love; we've been straddling it for too long. I'm done letting her believe the lies. In three weeks, our toes will be in the sands of St. Tropez and I'll be damned if it's as enemies.*"

Becca and I aren't enemies but I'm now acutely aware that we, too, have a deadline... an expiration date. I have three weeks to record her book, then I'll be back on a plane to California.

"He's going to be perfect for Bryan," one of the women coos, pulling me from my depressing thoughts. I'd correct her on the name change, but I leave that to Becca to address.

I glance at my watch. We have about an hour and a half before Becca can leave. I've made no plans for this evening and the clock is ticking. I excuse myself and head out of the ballroom, finding a quiet corridor to make a call.

Josh answers on the first ring. "Julian. To what do I owe the pleasure?"

"Money can only buy so much. I need access somewhere tomorrow. If I text you the info, can you make it happen?"

"Ask and you shall receive," he replies with a chuckle.

Once we hang up, I send him the info and research where to take my Becca tonight.

---

"Okay, you got me here. Will you finally tell me how the hell you can afford all this on a narrator's salary?" Becca takes a sip of wine and narrows her eyes at me.

I sigh and fiddle with the napkin in my lap. I really hate talking about money. Most women stay with me solely for the lifestyle. I don't think Becca is that way, but it's hard to divulge this kind of information to someone who is essentially a stranger. A beautiful stranger. But a stranger nonetheless; I've only known her a week. Taking her to one of the most expensive restaurants in the city probably was another hint at my wealth, but I wanted to treat her to an experience that she'd never forget. A rooftop terrace with incredible food and wine was a must.

"The simple answer is investments. The longer answer, I was part of a start-up in Silicon Valley and it took off. I let my buddy, Josh, buy me out. Now, I live comfortably and probably will for the rest of my life, as I'm smart with my money."

My answer has her nodding along in understanding. "So, you're some kind of secret billionaire and do audiobooks for funzies?"

"I don't feel comfortable telling you *exactly* how much I have, but I can say that I am well off and like to keep it secret. And audiobooks? It was something I always wanted to do. You know when you were a kid, and someone would ask you what you wanted to be when you grew up, before you understood the realities of the world and money? I wanted to narrate. I grew up listening to books on cassette and CD before audiobook apps existed. I loved how the voice actors brought the stories to life and I wanted to do the same." *Why am I telling her all this? Talk about word vomit. Rein it in, Evans.*

"I'm sorry. It was incredibly inappropriate for me to ask in the first place. I promise I won't bring it up again. I get how awkward it can be. When my books took off, it was always the first thing people would ask me." Becca pauses. "So, tell me about this vineyard you own in California. What varietals do you specialize in?" she asks with a smirk.

*Looks like my Becca did her homework.*

---

"Dinner was incredible. Thank you."

Becca's hand hasn't left mine since we entered the limo. I lift our joined hands to my lips, pressing a chaste kiss to her knuckles. "Pleasure is all mine, my Becca."

She chuckles. "Again with the *my Becca.*"

"You are. Even if you haven't admitted it to yourself yet." We're finally alone, except for our driver, so I'm tempted to do the one thing I've been itching to do since the hotel. I raise the partition and kneel in front of her.

"*Julian.* What are you doing?" Her eyes are wild and it eggs me on further.

I slide my hands up her legs under her dress, savoring her silky skin until I reach the top where her sexy thighs meet her hips. Her eyes dart around, as if we could get caught at any moment.

"No one can see us," I assure her. "Be my good girl and spread your legs for me."

Becca listens beautifully. I settle between her legs and lift up to kiss her, keeping one hand firmly in place on her thigh, and gripping the seat behind her with my other. It would be too easy to unzip my pants and slip inside her. The idea of taking her here makes my dick twitch.

My voice just above a whisper, I ask, "Is it okay if I touch you?" She nods. "With my tongue?" She nods again, biting her lip. I reach between her legs, pleased to find her already wet for me, even through her lacy underwear. "Take them off," I command. She hooks a finger into each side at her hips and slides them down her legs, kicking them off.

Her thighs press together. In a swift motion, I part them again and lower my face between her legs to devour her —just like I've been dreaming to do all night. The moment my tongue touches her clit, she lets out the sexiest fucking moan I've ever heard. She tastes too fucking good; I don't know how I'm going to work with her. I'll be craving her on my tongue the whole time.

I take my time teasing her. Her hands tangle in my hair, pulling me closer as she grinds on my mouth. I press two of my fingers inside her and, *fuck,* she's so tight and wet. She gasps as I curl my fingers inside her incredible unnamed pussy. I chuckle at the thought and the vibration is enough to make her come all over my face. It's the hottest thing I've experienced in my fucking life, feeling her pulse around my fingers as she moans my name.

*I'm fucking ruined.*

"That was…" Becca struggles to catch her breath.

"Oh, I'm not done with you yet. I want seconds." I drive my fingers deeper, forcing another moan from her. "You're going to give me one more before we get to the hotel. I warned you. You won't be walking for a week, *my Becca.*"

I've never wanted a woman as much as I want her. I'm torn between wanting to take my time and wanting to greedily consume her. She kisses me roughly, our tongues and teeth clashing, and I fucking love that this isn't one sided—she wants me as much as I want her and neither of us can get enough.

As much as I love kissing her, I want another taste of her coming on my tongue before we arrive. I lower myself between her legs and spread her wide to feast on her again, circling her clit and teasing every inch of her delicious cunt. I test different pressures to see what she likes; there's no reason to stick with one if I find four.

"It's too much," she moans.

I slow my pace and break long enough to tell her, "Are you going to be my good girl and come for me? Or... do I need to punish you later?"

Her breath catches. "Holy shit, you're into that? I don't know if I—"

"Becca," I interrupt. "I'd never hurt you. I'd do just about anything to bring you pleasure, to hear you moan my name again. Name it and I'll do it." She lets out a sigh of relief and I go right back to work on her beautiful pussy, nipping at her clit just enough to make her yelp. It quickly turns into a soft whimper. Time is not on my side. I suck hard on her clit and graze my teeth against it, curling my fingers right where she needs me. Her hips buck up, seeking more from me and I deliver. Within moments, she shatters for me, screaming my name and coming harder than the first time. I savor every fucking drop of her as she comes down from her orgasm.

"I can't move," Becca whines with a satisfied smile. She sags against the seat and I kiss the inside of her thigh. Peeling her dress down from around her waist, I'm grateful she picked the black dress that can hide the mess we just made. I tuck her lacy underwear in my pocket—she's not going to need them. "How do you expect me to ever have sex with another man after *that?*"

"We didn't have sex, Becca. That was just an appetizer."

## 14

## JULIAN

When we arrive at the hotel, she moves to open the door, but I take her other hand to stop her. With a quick shake of my head, I release her hand, with the understanding between us that there's no way in hell I'll let her open her own door. The driver gets out at the same time, but I'm quicker, rounding the back of the limo before he can get to her. He chuckles and, with a nod, heads back to the driver's seat. I open her door and offer her my hand.

"Such a gentleman," Becca quips.

"Hardly," I reply, kissing her knuckles.

I keep her hand in mine and lead us to the hotel elevators. I count no less than ten men who eye her as we cross the lobby. I thought for sure she would pull her hand away, but she must still be high from coming because she hasn't figured out that I'm claiming her as mine for everyone to see.

There's a comfortable silence between us as we wait for the illuminated numbers to count down from 36. Unfortunately, the comfortable part of the silence is cut short as I become lost in thought.

*Am I okay with this being casual? No. Will I be able to work with her and not want to touch her? No. Am I falling for a woman who is basically a stranger…? Fuck.*

Becca squeezes my hand once, pulling me from my freak out. "Are you okay?"

"Absolutely." I smile at her, melting at the sight of her captivating green eyes. They haunt me when I'm not with her. I'm about to divulge my feelings when the elevator doors open with a loud ding.

We step in and I press the number to my floor. My internal conflict must be written all over my face when Becca asks, "Are you sure? You look like you've seen a ghost. *Shit.*" She shakes her head. "You're already regretting this, aren't you? I knew us working together and sleeping together wasn't the best idea. I'm sorry if I made you uncomfortable."

I take her face in my hands and bring her lips to mine. She sighs against me. I trail kisses along her jaw and pull her closer, relishing the feeling of her bare back against my hand. I nip at the shell of her ear and insist, "I've been chasing you since the moment I laid eyes on you. There isn't a single moment with you that I've regretted. I just—" The elevator door opens before I can confess what I really want from her. *Fucking elevator.*

"You just what?" Becca presses the button to close the elevator doors and pulls the emergency stop. The elevator bounces once, causing both of us to momentarily lose our balance. She looks back at me expectantly as lights flash around us.

"Are you needing a book-worthy moment, *Merlot?*" Her breath catches as I kiss her cheek. "You want to know why my chest tightens every time I'm in your presence? What makes my palm itch to touch you? What's consumed my thoughts since the moment I took your hand on that plane and a fucking jolt of electricity coursed through my body?" I pause, taking all of her in —her pouty red lips, her fascinating emerald eyes, and a dusting of light brown freckles peeping through her makeup. She's fucking stunning, but it doesn't compare to her beautiful heart that I want to steal for myself. "I don't want you tonight, my Becca. I want you tomorrow, and the next day, *and* the next."

I swallow hard, fear creeping in that she doesn't feel this, too. All I know is that, by some cosmic happenstance, we met… and now I need her, want her, and am going to do everything in my power to keep her.

"How can you be so sure?" she asks, her breath shaky.

"I'm not. The absurdity of it all should have me on the next flight to California. Instead, I'm here, begging for a chance to see where this goes."

"If anyone found out…" Becca's voice trails off but her eyes never leave mine.

"They won't."

Her eyes dart between mine. She sucks in a short breath, exhaling as if she's about to counter me. She doesn't.

Instead, she reaches down and presses the emergency stop button. The elevator doors open but neither of us move. They close again and it begins to descend.

"Okay," she whispers, breaking the silence. "We can't be seen together, not like this. Not until the recordings are done. It was already too risky going to dinner together."

"Always the voice of reason," I tease, but hope fills my chest. If it were up to me, I'd have her in my bed every night until I go home. After reviewing the script, I'd be lucky if I could prolong this for a month. Two would be excessive. Three would be impossible.

*Maybe she'll come to California with me? No, that's ridiculous...* *Right?*

I take her chin between my thumb and forefinger and bring her lips to mine before she changes her mind. She whimpers against my lips.

"What have you done to me, my Becca?" The elevator doors open. "Want to go have an adventure?" I don't wait for her answer; I take her hand, guiding her out of the hotel and onto the busy New York streets.

"Where are we going?"

"You'll see."

Becca pauses then asks, "How long?"

"How long will you give me?"

She takes out her phone, scrolling and tapping various apps before replying, "48 hours."

On the ride to the airport, we stop at her apartment. I've given her no clues as to where we are going. I had plans for us to leave in the morning but if I want to be openly with her, I need it to be where no one knows who she is. She runs upstairs, changes into comfortable clothing, and grabs her passport. I don't want to give away my surprise by telling her what to pack, so I'll order clothes to be delivered to the hotel when we arrive.

"You really aren't going to tell me where we're going?" She buckles her lap belt, looking up at me through her lashes.

"Nope," I reply, popping the 'p.' "Trust me?"

"I'm not sure," she replies, unable to hide her amusement. "A man I met a week ago whisks me off on a charter plane to an unknown destination. Sounds to me like the beginning of a dark mafia romance where a woman's taken by some hot crime lord. Only, plot twist, she's way too excited to go." I turn before I give myself away. I would totally whisk her away and keep her for myself like some sort of mafia don if it wouldn't kill her to be away from her work.

*How can things be this easy with someone I hardly know?*

Only a week ago, I sat down next to her, just like this. What is the likelihood that the most beautiful woman in the world, who's smart as a whip, would give me the time of day? Without knowing about my wealth? I shake my head in disbelief. Lost in thought, I'm surprised when her hand takes mine.

It's the perfect fit. *She's* the perfect fit.

The flight is several hours and, with it already being a late night, we both close our eyes and let sleep claim us. A few hours later, the flight attendant stirs me. "Sir, we are halfway to our destination. Would you or your"— she glances at Becca—"like anything?"

"We're fine, thank you," I reply, looking down at my Becca. She's cuddled up against my arm and shoulder. Once the flight attendant walks away, I kiss Becca on the forehead, letting my lips linger for just a moment.

*Mine.*

Another five or so hours later, the plane begins its descent, and I wake her. "Becca," I whisper, "we're almost there."

She groans. "Where are…?"

"St. Tropez," I finish. Becca sits up straight in alarm. "I thought it would be—" My words are cut off with a kiss. I'm thankful this isn't a commercial flight as she groans into my mouth, hungry for me. An involuntary growl erupts from my chest, and I resist the urge to strip her down and bury my face between her legs again. "If you keep kissing me like that, I'm going to take you right here, right now."

She smiles against my lips as she replies, "Is that a promise?"

*Fuck, I forgot she's got fire in her.*

"You think that seatbelt sign will stop me, my Becca?" She pulls back, just an inch, and I already miss the taste of her. "Get back here." I glide my hand into her hair and bring her mouth back where it belongs. She melts into me the moment our lips touch. I'm too busy enjoying kissing her to notice her hands wandering. It isn't until she grips my belt that I'm tearing her hand away and kissing the inside of her wrist. "Later. I want to finish what I started first."

Becca fists my shirt and brings me closer, our lips a breath apart. "You brought me to France?"

"Yes."

"I… I wrote it in one of my books because I've never been." Her voice catches and I want to take her in my arms and never let go. "You…" She kisses me again.

"Are you ready for"—I check my watch—"thirty-twoish hours with me on the beach?"

She shakes her head, biting her lip. "I don't care about the beach, Julian. This is the most… I'm speechless." Closing the distance, she kisses me softly. "Thank you."

## 15

---

## BECCA

Fuck. I like him. I like him a lot. I meant what I said, I couldn't care less about the beach or France; Julian could have taken me to a swap meet and I would have been happy just spending time with him. This whole "taking me to the other side of the world" thing is beyond words.

We walk into the resort lobby to check in. The room promises a city view, and while I can't wait to dip my toes in the sand, I know the view of St. Tropez is going to be spectacular. The beach is a quick walk from here, so I won't be missing out.

The old elevator takes us up a few floors. By the time we reach the suite, the anticipation is killing me. Julian unlocks the door and, as it swings open, the glass patio door across the room offers me a glimpse of the view. I make a beeline for it.

This is the view I envisioned when I wrote my book. This is what my characters saw in *Vacation with the Enemy*. I fight back the tears prickling behind my eyes—it's so fucking beautiful. The buildings are neutral in color but most roofs are a beautiful dark sienna. The sunlight bounces off them, giving a stark contrast to the clear blue water behind them.

"Julian, you have to see—" My words are cut short when two strong arms embrace me from behind. "It's gorgeous… and don't you dare say something cheesy to ruin this moment."

He chuckles and kisses my shoulder. "I wouldn't dream of it."

I turn in his arms and plant my palms on his chest. "This has to be a dream. Yesterday, I was two drinks away from needing someone to hold my hair back at a book conference. Today, I'm in France with a man I was certain wanted someone else." He frowns and I explain, "Ingrid."

Julian barks out a laugh. "You're serious? Not only is Ingrid one of my friends from years ago, she's…" He doesn't finish his sentence, presumably to not out his friend's sexuality.

"Not into men? Yeah, I figured that out. Her girlfriend was on the panel with me. It just"—I chew on my lip— "it looked like more. I was dealing with the whole 'Bryan panel' thing and, when I looked out into the crowd… I'm sorry I assumed."

"Apology not accepted. I know what it looked like; Ingrid even pointed it out. It's not your fault, it's on me. I'm an affectionate person with people I care about," he sighs. "That includes you. I'm crazy about you, Becca. I gladly uprooted my life to be near someone I knew for less than a day. I'd do it again, if it meant I got to spend more time with you."

"Why are we in St. Tropez?" I blurt out, ignoring his declaration.

It takes him by surprise but shrugs. "Why not?"

"Did you know this is where one of my books is set?"

"I did." Julian smirks.

"Who *are* you?" I ask, mostly to myself.

"For someone who hates answering questions, you sure do love asking them," he teases.

The flecks of gold in his eyes are burrowing into every inch of my soul. I can't look away, for fear that he'll steal a piece of it if I do. I have nothing more to say. All at once, something snaps in both of us, the silence broken when our mouths crash into each other.

I'm overcome with the burning desire to have this man naked. Now. His hands roam my body and it only intensifies my need for him. He cups my ass and slides his hands down to my thighs, pulling them up and around his waist. His lips never leave mine as he walks us into the room and lays me down on the bed.

Our breathing heavy, I ask, "Did you by chance bring condoms?"

Julian's wide eyes are enough confirmation, but he still replies, "I didn't bring you here for this, so I didn't think to bring any."

"None in your wallet?"

He chuckles and presses his forehead to mine. "No. No cliché wallet condom. I just got out of a serious relationship. I know you think I'm a flirt but I don't sleep around."

"That's not… I don't think—"

"I know, I'm just being honest." A sly smirk tugs at his lips as he lowers himself down my body. "I don't need to be inside you to enjoy every inch of your incredible body. I've been craving another taste of you since I stepped foot out of that limo."

"As amazing as you are with that talented tongue of yours, you can't just keep going down on me. I'll become spoiled and you'll need to service me on the daily."

Julian slips off my leggings and panties. Unlike in the limo, he takes his time, torturing me. "If I spent the rest of my life with my face between your legs, I'd die a happy man. I'll admit, I love the idea of you wanting me as much as I want you." He nips at my thigh, making me yelp. "You craving my touch." His hands glide up my legs until they reach my inner thigh and he spreads me wide. I gasp. "Wishing I was tasting every inch of you." He trails kisses up to my hip. Close, but not where I desperately need him. He swipes his knuckle over my clit, forcing a moan from me. "Wanting me inside you, not feeling whole unless I've painted the walls of your delicious cunt with my own release."

"Julian," I whimper.

"Yes, my Becca?" He smiles as he kisses an inch above my pussy.

"Please."

"Please, what, baby?" He continues kissing me everywhere… except where I want him. It's deliciously frustrating.

"Please touch me."

Julian chuckles. "Where do you want me to touch you?" I groan. "What? You're the writer. Tell me. Where do you want me to start?" He moves up between my legs, kissing up my stomach. I lift my shirt and he tugs it off me, tossing it to the ground. He unhooks my bra and slowly pulls down the straps, kissing every inch of my shoulders as he removes it. "Fuck. You're so damn beautiful, my Becca."

"You're wearing too many clothes."

"It appears I am." Julian looks down at his shirt and back to me. "Don't change the subject. Where do you want me to touch you?" His dimples on full display; he's enjoying his little game far too much. I can't help but indulge him as he continues his quest to tease me. "Should I start here?" He traces his finger from my ear, down my neck, to my collar bone. "Or perhaps here?"

His featherlight touch continues down my chest, swiping his thumb across one of my incredibly taut nipples. He takes the other in his mouth for just a moment—a quick nip. My breathing is shaky and I shudder beneath him.

He hums. "As much as I love teasing you, I need to be inside you tonight. You're going to jump in the shower and I'm going to run to the store and grab the largest fucking box of condoms the world has ever seen." We both laugh and he kisses down my stomach, still slow and gentle. I close my eyes, savoring his touch. He presses one last kiss to my belly. "Come on. You've been traveling all day. Go relax. I'll be back in a bit."

I fist his shirt and bring his face within an inch of mine. "Not so fast, mister. You're not going to rile me up like that and not finish what you started."

"I absolutely am," he replies, brushing his nose against mine. "But tell you what, I'll join you for a quick shower before I head out."

I release him and he kisses my cheek. I pad off to the bathroom, looking behind me once to find a still very clothed Julian.

As I turn on the water, his arm snakes around my waist, pulling me to him. "Do you know how hard it is to not touch you?" he murmurs against my shoulder as he kisses it softly.

"I don't know, how hard is it?" I reach behind me and grab his cock through his pants. He groans and bites down gently on my shoulder. A whimper escapes me.

*Fuck, he's thick. This thing is going to break me in half.*

I test the water—it's now the perfect temperature, extra hot, just how I like it. I haven't even seen him shirtless and the suspense is too much. I shimmy out of his hold, spin around, look him up and down expectantly, then playfully ask, "Do you plan on getting your clothes wet?"

Julian strips down faster than a teenager in a locker room. *Holy fucking shit.* It's like every inch of him is chiseled from stone. I know I'm gawking at this Adonis of a man but I can't help it. I'm so wound up from his touch that I want to climb him like a tree. My gaze travels lower and—

"My eyes are up here, Becca," he says with a smirk.

"No, they aren't." I can't stop staring. "How on earth do you expect that to fit? I haven't had sex in… I don't fucking remember." My eyes finally meet his. "No fucking way." I write about book boyfriends with giant cocks, but this non-fictional man puts them all to shame.

He guides me into the shower and closes the distance, sliding his hand into my hair. I anticipate his kiss but it never comes. "While I appreciate the praise, I know you can take it." My breath catches.

Julian kisses me, teasing my mouth to open for him. It's slow at first but his sweet and sensual movements are quickly replaced by a beastly desire. He drives two of his fingers inside me with little warning, making me scream out. I don't have time to process the fullness when he moves down my body, kneeling before me. He grabs my leg and slings it over his shoulder and, in an instant, his mouth is on my clit, his tongue swirling in tight circles. There isn't an ounce of tenderness in his touch. It's rough and demanding. I'm being devoured.

"Eyes on me, Becca," he growls into my pussy. I don't dare look, it's already too much. "I want you to watch as you take four of my fingers like my good girl. I need to stretch you out, baby, but don't worry, I'll work you up to it."

My eyes snap down to him. "*Four?*" I shriek. "Are you out of your mind?"

He chuckles against me as he sucks hard on my clit. I'm already moments from coming but he slows his pace, my orgasm no longer in reach. "Doubt me again and I won't let you come." He slips another finger inside and I wince. "Fuck, baby, you feel so good. You're going to feel amazing stretched around my cock."

My clit is swollen and I'm aching to come. "Please," I beg.

"Please, what, baby?"

"Please let me come." My words come out strangled. He adds a fourth finger and I'm entirely too full.

"I knew you were made for this, so fucking perfect." He sucks on my clit as he massages the walls of my pussy. My orgasm builds but I need more pressure. I grind against his mouth, pulling him closer. "So greedy. I fucking love it." I fall apart at his words and come harder than I have in my life. Julian holds me in place as he slowly pulls his fingers out, leaving me feeling empty. If he let go, I'd crumple to a heap in the shower.

"I told you. You can't keep going down on me," I say breathlessly.

He stands and kisses me roughly. I taste myself as his tongue sweeps across mine, making me want him to push deep inside me. I have an IUD and I'm clean… it would be so easy.

"I'll taste you whenever I please, my Becca."

*Fuck, that's hot. Who the fuck is this guy, waltzing in here like he owns my pussy?*

"I haven't even touched you. Every time I want to, your face is between my legs again." I can barely get the words out.

He chuckles, biting his lip. "There's all the time in the world for that."

"What are you talking about? You'll be gone when you're done with the audiobook in a few weeks, maybe a month."

"Not if I can help it."

I frown. "What is that supposed to mean?"

"Let me worry about that." He brushes wet strands of hair off my shoulder and leans in to kiss me. I stop him with my fingers on his lips.

"Oh, no. You're not getting out of this one. Are you going to sabotage the project, to prolong your stay?"

"Of course not." He frowns. "I would never do anything to hurt you or your writing career. If I wanted to stay, I would simply get a place in New York. I'll admit, part of why I don't want you touching me is that it'll be one step closer to being inside you. Once I've had you, I don't know that I'll ever be able to go back to California."

## 16

---

## JULIAN

"We've only known each other a week, Julian. How can you consider moving?"

I grab a washcloth and lather soap on it before slowly dragging it down every inch of her body. I don't reply to her question but she also doesn't protest or push further, instead just letting me wash her. I have this unexplainable carnal need to take care of her, to worship *all* of her, this beautiful stranger of mine.

*Is this some soulmate shit? It feels like something out of a movie or a book. Fuck, I only know her real last name because of the contract. Am I actually considering moving for her?*

*Yes. Yes, I fucking am.*

Becca's hand cups my cheek, pulling me from whatever the fuck that was. Moving isn't out of the question, but it shouldn't be on the table either.

"Hey," she says softly. I cover her hand, pulling it to my lips and kissing her palm, never taking my eyes off hers.

"Don't do something impulsive. Whatever this is, it's intense, but you can't consider moving across the country for a woman you don't know. Plus, you never know, I could be the worst lay of your life and then you'd be stuck with me." She fails to keep a straight face and it's the most endearing thing I've witnessed in my life.

"I'd see for myself right now, but I need to run to the store first." As much as I want to drive into her bare, I've been burned before by women who lied about being on the pill or other birth control in an attempt to get knocked up and walk away with a decent check. I don't think Becca's like that, but as she said, it's only been a week. I'm pretty sure I felt an IUD while I fingered her but I was more focused on her pleasure than checking for birth control.

She bites her lip. "You don't... you don't have to go if you don't want to."

"I can't. It's not you, Becca." I kiss her softly. "I trust you. I'm just—"

"No need to explain. Whatever it is, it's important to you. We'll use protection. I'm also fine showing you my online medical chart to prove when I had my IUD done and the last time I was tested. You know, as a back up for when your fucking monster cock tears through the condom."

*Could she be any more fucking perfect?*

"You're really okay with it?" I ask.

"Why the hell wouldn't I? Do you know how much research I've had to do for my books? I'm sure the FBI has had a field day looking through my browser history. Nothing you could say would shock me. Turn me on? Absolutely. If this is a boundary for you, it's sexy as fuck that you are okay talking about it."

I shut off the water, kiss her cheek, and storm out of the shower. I need to claim this woman, once and for all.

"Shit. I'm sorry. Was it something I said?" Becca steps out and I wrap her in a towel, not caring that I'm still dripping wet.

"There isn't a single thing wrong... well, there's one thing but I'm about to remedy that." I pull her to me, loving the feel of her slick naked body against mine. "You're fucking perfect, Becca. I'm about to make good on my promises."

"Oh, fuck. I'm about to be broken in half, aren't I?"

"Where's the fun in that? I can't play with that pretty unnamed pussy of yours if I break you, can I?" I drag the towel down her body to dry her off, then quickly dry my hair before tossing the towel to the ground.

"Well, now that we've confirmed that I won't be split in half like a log on one of those lumberjack thirst traps, I'll see you back here in ten." She faces the mirror, ties her hair up, and uses her fingertips to wipe away her smudged mascara.

I'm flooded with images of her on her knees, choking on my cock, her eyes watering and mascara smeared just like this as she takes all of me in her mouth. Fuck. I'm hard again.

*I can wait ten minutes.*

I blow out a deep breath. *How is she so fucking cool about all of this?*

"Ten minutes," I confirm.

Rummaging through my suitcase for fresh clothes, I pick out a pair of khaki cargo shorts, boxer briefs, and a black tee. I get dressed the fastest I have in my life. When I turn back, Becca's made herself comfortable on the bed in a fluffy white robe with an e-reader. I grab my wallet from my other pants and stuff it in my front pocket. I don't trust things in my back pocket while traveling.

I make my way to the bed and sit on the side. I'm about to kiss her goodbye, but she stops me with her fingers against my lips, not lifting her gaze from reading. "I'll see you in ten minutes, Julian. Never interrupt a woman while she's in the middle of a spicy scene." I kiss her palm—one of my favorite places to kiss her now—and make my way off the bed.

There's a store a few doors down that should have what I need. I feel like a bit of a dick coming back with only a club store sized box of rubbers, so I pop into the wine shop across the street to grab a few bottles of local varietals.

*Do I get flowers? No, that's fucking weird. Get it together, Julian.*

I pick up a bouquet of orange and pink roses despite

myself, that I will now always consider to be "fuck me" flowers.

While I make my way back to the hotel, I come to my senses. I need all of her, but if I want to be with her, I need to step up my game. Yes, I brought her to France, but after I make love to her until the sun rises, I'm going to take her out to explore the city.

As I pass the lobby check-in, I drop off the "fuck me" flowers—that make me look like a douche—to the front desk, and head up to the room.

When I enter, I call out, "Sorry I took so long, I—" I clamp my mouth shut when I realize she's peacefully asleep, curled up under the covers.

Becca startles as I approach the bed. "Hey, you're back. Okay, let the sexy time commence," she says through a yawn.

I kiss her forehead. "No, baby, get your rest."

"Oh, thank fuck. I'm exhausted after you practically put your whole hand up my... *lady garden*."

"It wasn't my whole hand. Don't exaggerate, *Merlot*." I strip off my shorts and slide into bed with her, pleasantly surprised to find her completely naked beneath the sheets. I want to feel her against me so I take my shirt off and throw it on top of my shorts on the ground. "Come here." I offer my arm for her to snuggle up next to me.

"Oh, we're cuddling now?" Becca raises an eyebrow.

"Absolutely. Get over here."

She chuckles and I wrap her in my arms, her legs tangled with mine. Fuck, she feels so good. My heart was shattered when my ex and I broke up, but it's as if none of it even happened since I met Becca. There isn't an ounce of sadness left in my chest. I'm present in this moment, loving her soft body pressed against mine. I graze my fingers up and down her back, listening to her breathing as it slows.

"Hey, baby. Before you fall asleep, what sounds good for dinner?" I ask. "I'll order it so it'll be here when we wake up."

"Don't you think it's a little soon to be calling a stranger *baby?*"

"Does it bother you?"

"No," she replies sleepily.

"Then, I don't intend to stop."

Becca yawns. "I suppose it's better than *my Becca.*"

"I have no intention of stopping that, either, because you are."

"If you say so," she sighs and falls asleep shortly after.

A few minutes later, I doze off. I'm not sure how long I'm asleep when I feel Becca shifting away from me. When I don't immediately spoon up behind her, she grabs my arm and pulls it around her. I chuckle and kiss her shoulder.

"What's so funny?" she asks, her voice half muffled by the pillow.

"Nothing," I reply, unable to wipe the smile off my face.

"Liar." Becca grinds her ass against my cock.

*Two can play that game.*

I grab her thigh and pull it over me, giving me full access to reach between her legs and rub slow circles around her clit. "Already so wet for me." She lets out a breathy moan and reaches her arm behind to cup my neck and tangle her fingers in my hair. "Are you going to be my good girl and come fast and hard on my hand for me, so I can take you from behind, just like this?"

"Please," she whimpers.

"Please what, baby?"

"Break me in half."

I nip at her ear. "I already told you, there will be no breaking. By the time I'm through with you, you won't want to be touched by anyone other than me, ever again." I slip off my underwear and return my fingers to her pussy, rubbing my cock up and down her slit without pushing inside. As I continue teasing her clit, her breathing becomes heavier. I dip two fingers inside her, then a third, making her gasp.

"Is that… a promise?" She struggles to speak.

"You're mine. My Becca. My beautiful stranger. I want every piece of you that you'll give me." I kiss her shoulder before removing my fingers from her tight pussy, bringing them to my mouth to suck them clean. "One second, baby." Reaching behind me, I grab a condom and tear the foil with my teeth before carefully removing it and rolling it onto my cock. "You're going to take every inch and show me who this delicious cunt belongs to."

Becca whimpers at my words but it's cut short as I slowly push inside her, just an inch. "Julian," she moans. I push in another, my fingers playing with her clit. She's so tight, it's taking her a while to adjust to me. It feels too damn good. If I'm not careful, I'll come too quickly.

"You're doing amazing. Look at you taking me so well. Your pussy was made for me, baby." I push in another two inches, making her cry out in pleasure. She pushes back into me, taking another inch. I bite down gently on her shoulder and kiss her neck. "You still owe me what's mine before I fuck you." I push in to the hilt and she tries to rock against me.

"What's yours?" she asks breathlessly.

"You, baby. I'm not moving until you come for me."

"It's too much," she breathes.

"You can take it." I circle her clit faster, making her tighten around me. It's too much for *me*. "I know you're close. Push back on my cock and grind onto it." She does as I asked and fuck, it feels incredible. "Just like that." She lets out a loud moan. I thrust deeper inside her and hold. She clenches and, within seconds, her pussy's pulsing and she's writhing in my arms as she comes. "That's it, baby. Fuck, you did so well. I'm going to take at least one more from you, are you ready?"

She nods and whispers, "Yes."

"Attagirl." I tease her with shallow thrusts, hitting right where she needs me. She's greedy and takes more of me with each push into her. I pick up my pace but don't allow myself deep inside her. I'm too close and need to take my time. I knew sleeping with her would be the best sex of my life, but I didn't anticipate it feeling like this— consumed with my need for her and fueled by her wanting me as much as I want her.

She grips the nape of my neck. "I need more." I drive up into her, harder each time, but still not giving her all of me. "Yes, right there. Don't stop."

I wrap my arm around her waist and use the leverage to finally push all the way inside her again. Becca cries out my name and reaches down to take my hand still gripping her. "Doing okay, baby?"

"You feel so good. I'm close. Come with me?"

"Okay, hold on." I pick up my pace, careful to not hurt her. I'm worried I didn't stretch her out nearly enough; I just couldn't take another moment not being inside her. A few more thrusts and she screams my name. Feeling her come on my cock is unlike anything I've ever experienced. My own release follows the moment she surprises me by twisting her body just enough to pull me in to kiss her.

We lie there for several moments, exploring each other's mouths and tasting each other as if we have all the time in the world. I make no move to pull out of her. That wasn't just sex, it was something else entirely and I've never come so hard in my life.

This beautiful stranger of mine has me under her spell, but it's one I hope with all my being is never broken.

# 17

# BECCA

I don't stop kissing him. If I distract myself, I don't have to come to terms with the fact that I just had mind blowing sex with a man who will leave in a few weeks. I know he joked that he would stay, but my heart couldn't take it if I fell for him, only to have to watch him go.

Julian pulls out slowly and I'm aching to have him inside me again. "I'll be right back," he says with a final kiss to my shoulder. He heads to the bathroom to discard the condom, leaving me staring at the ceiling, alone with my thoughts.

*How am I supposed to have the best sex of my life and move on as if it never happened?*

*This man brought a woman he hardly knows clear across the globe because it was the setting of her book.*

*Fuck he's hot and that cock of his... oof.*

*Stay focused, Becs.*

*Who is this guy? And what the hell does he want with someone like me?*

*Maybe I was right and he's some sort of secret billionaire? I know he said he's well off but…*

*No, that's ridiculous.*

*I really do need to write a book about this…*

"Did I break you, my Becca?"

I turn my head, finding Julian leaning against the bathroom door frame with his arms crossed. "Break me? Not physically, no," I admit.

Julian chuckles and pushes off the frame. "Are you hungry? Room service should be here in half an hour." He stalks toward me like an underwear model on the runway who lost their panties halfway down the catwalk —confident but cautious.

Climbing back onto the bed, he rips the comforter off me. The cold air causes my nipples to stand at attention… or maybe it's just the sexy as fuck man who whisked me off to France for the most delicious orgasms I've ever experienced. My initial reaction is to cover up but he's seen me naked so I let go of my insecurities.

*Fuck it. Let him see all of me, imperfections and all.*

"So, uh, what did you order for us?"

"You'll find out after I have my appetizer…"

The sand is soft beneath my toes as the warm breeze whips around me. After Julian made me come countless times and we ate, he suggested we watch the sunset on the beach.

He bought me a one and a two-piece bathing suit so I could pick whatever I'd be most comfortable in. My tits look amazing in both of them, so I go with the black two-piece, knowing he won't be able to take his hands off me with extra skin showing.

"It was a mistake."

Frowning, I ask, "What was?" *Please, don't say this trip... It's fucking magical. Don't burst my bubble!*

"Buying you that." His gaze roams my body. "Come on, let's get you in the water. If I have to window shop that body of yours any longer, I'm going to claim you right here on this beach."

"Wait, what the fuck do you mean 'window shopping?'" I ask as he drags me into the water. "*Oh, fuck!* That's cold." We're only in to our knees but it's still a shock to the senses.

Julian pulls me to him. "Window shopping. You know, looking but not touching... or taking you home with me." He cups my cheek and grazes the pad of his thumb across my bottom lip before kissing me. He growls in response to the moan that escapes me and glides his hand into my hair, carefully tugging to move me exactly where he wants me.

Being here with Julian is comfortable, like we've been doing this for years, not a week.

One. Fucking. Week. In seven days, he's turned my world upside down.

The waves crashing around us are the only thing keeping me from feeling like this is all just a dream. I can see myself falling for him if I'm not careful.

"Julian," I whisper against his lips.

"Yes, baby."

I chuckle and pull back, just an inch. "How fast are you?"

"I ran a half marathon last year. Why?"

"Because I am going to swim in the waters of St. Tropez and, if you catch me, you won't need to window shop." I lower my voice, even though there isn't a soul in sight. "I'm going to skinny dip in France."

I shrug out of his hold and run into the cool water. It's like jumping into a swimming pool as a kid—you're better off with a cannon ball than dipping your toe in.

I only make it waist deep before he's wrapped his arms around me from behind. I turn in his arms. "Damn it, you're fast. I thought I would've at least made it to my shoulders."

Julian laughs, his eyes crinkling at the sides. The sunlight makes the gold flecks stand out more than usual.

*Usual? What the hell am I saying?*

"Don't you think I've chased you enough?"

Wrapping my arms around his neck, I press my cheek to

his and whisper, "You have, but I enjoy it far too much, *my Julian*."

He pulls back, the laughter gone and replaced with a heat in his gaze that would make any woman drop her panties. "Do you believe in love at first sight?"

My breath catches. "Oh, um, the correct answer as a romance author is *yes, of course*."

He smirks but his eyes are still burning into me. "So, Merlot does, but what about Becca?"

"I didn't." I chew on my lip, hoping he won't continue this line of questioning. I can't fall for him.

*I could always visit California...*

"Me either." He kisses me softly. "But maybe I should. It would explain a lot."

"Next you'll tell me we're fated mates. Don't be getting all romantic on me, sir. We only have a few weeks of... whatever this is. Then you're back to your winery in California."

Julian unhooks the clasp on the back of my top. "I'll be as romantic as I want to be. I'm obsessed with a woman I hardly know."

He unties the swimsuit around my neck and, as the top falls, he stuffs it in the pocket of his swim trunks; his eyes never leaving mine. He runs his hands up my sides. I want him to touch me so fucking bad, but he avoids everywhere I really need him.

"You said you were going to skinny dip." Julian bites his lip and hooks his fingers in each side of the bottoms, pulling them down. I step out of them and he places them in his other pocket.

"How do you *always* get me naked and you're still fully clothed?" I playfully ask.

"You're fucking exquisite. I want to appreciate every inch of you. Last time I checked, I don't need my clothes off to do that."

"Aren't you worried someone might see me?"

"There isn't another soul for at least a mile. I made sure of it." He clears his throat. "I mean, see for yourself. I could take you hard and fast, making you scream for more. No one would hear you."

"As hot as that is, it also sounds a little like the plot of a thriller or murder mystery: romance author murdered in the waters of St. Tropez by her lover."

Julian lets out a hearty laugh. "I suppose it does sound a little murdery, doesn't it?" He kisses me, smiling against my lips. "I fucking adore you."

As light as the mood is, his words weigh heavily on my heart. This is the equivalent of a hot summer fling. The audiobook will be recorded, we'll part ways, and I won't have this attentive, sweet, funny, and sexy as sin man in my life anymore. I should enjoy him while he's here. He isn't Bryan; he's not going to run off with the female narrator and then try to ride my coattails as I climb the charts with my next novel. But... we're burning daylight. We have a few weeks before I have to let him go.

And so, pushing aside any sadness for a loss I haven't yet experienced, I go for my naked swim. This is a once in a lifetime opportunity. When will I get the chance again to be on a secluded beach and feel free like this? Never. The answer is fucking never. I savor the feel of the crisp water and bask in the sun that's slowly moving to the horizon, the rays bouncing off Julian's golden skin. Out here, he looks like some sort of mythical god—a sexy Poseidon.

The sun's almost set and, thankfully, Julian hasn't continued his romantic declarations. We make our way out of the water to our towels on the beach and, for a moment, I nearly forgot I'm naked. Julian pulls out the swim bottoms from his trunks, then reaches into his other pocket to pull out my top, only to pause. His eyes wide, he looks out to the water and back to me.

"Fuck, I'm so fucking sorry. Your top… I don't know what happened, it must have slipped out of my pocket out there." He dries the bottoms with a towel and hands them to me.

I double over in laughter. "You totally just threw it out there so you could stare at my tits a little longer, didn't you?"

Julian wraps a towel behind me and pulls me to him. "No, my Becca. If I wanted you naked, I wouldn't need to throw away a swimsuit." He leans in, his breath tickling my ear as he lowers his voice and says, "I'd only need to ask."

"And you think I'd drop my panties? Just like that?"

He nips at my ear and kisses my neck. "You would. Just as you could have me on my knees for you any time you wanted. In fact, it's been entirely too long since I've had my face between your legs. We should get back."

"I was promised a sunset," I insist as he tries to lead us away from the beach.

A smirk tugs at his lips. "Well, who says you can't have both?" He pulls at my towel and lays it on the sand carefully. "You'll get your sunset and I'll get to hear you scream my name as you come for me. Lay down, baby. I've window shopped long enough."

## 18

---

## JULIAN

Becca gave me 48 hours. I kept my word.

How is it that, after only a week with her, I'm throwing all caution to the wind? Katrina and I broke up a couple weeks ago and here I am wooing this goddess of a woman as if my entire relationship never happened.

The flight home is both too short and too long—I want to prolong this alone time with her, but the quicker we get back, the quicker my contract is up and I can openly date her. When I asked if she believed in love at first sight, I wasn't being glib. She captivated me from the moment I laid eyes on her. If I still feel this way in a few weeks, there's no way in hell I'm going back to California.

We're flying commercial home and I was able to get two first class seats next to each other. I really wanted to spend more time just being together since we left, but my dick had other plans. The majority of our trip was spent naked, so a charter plane was out of the question

—too much of a temptation to join the mile high club. I'll have to bring her back to St. Tropez to see more than the inside of a hotel room.

Since we entered the airport, Becca hasn't let me touch her at all, even to hold her hand. I understand her concerns, and I don't want to jeopardize anything with her book, but not touching her feels… wrong. I highly doubt we'd be recognized, but I'd rather her be comfortable than risk driving her away.

A few hours into the flight, she's spent most of her time reading on her e-reader, while I'm reading a physical copy of her book and annotating.

"What are your plans for tomorrow?" I keep my voice low and intentionally make sure it comes out sultry.

Her breath catches. "I, uh, need to wrap up a few things after the conference."

"Can I see you tomorrow night?"

Becca chews on her lip. I want to take that lip between my teeth and kiss her hard, if she'd let me. "That's not the best idea. We shouldn't be seen together in New York." She sounds almost sad, which gives me hope. She still wants to see me, but she's worried about getting caught.

"What if I come by your place?"

"Maybe…"

"I'll come by around seven. I'll bring dinner."

She shakes her head, chuckling and returning her attention to her e-reader. "You've been inside me for the entire trip. I think you can go one night without fucking me, Julian."

I lift her chin to face me, discovering that her emerald eyes are full of heat. I lean in, leaving only an inch between us. "That is exactly why I should come by. I spent the last couple days worshiping your body, don't you think it's time I enjoy all the other parts of you? I promise I'll keep my hands to myself." I close the distance. She moans the moment my lips touch hers and I capture it by deepening our kiss.

Becca breaks away far too quickly for my liking. "There's no way you're coming by. I don't want to be tempted. I'll see you in two days for recordings." A blush creeps up her cheeks.

"Why don't I practice right now?"

She chuckles and I set down my paperback to pull up a different title of hers on my phone. I don't know how much of *Delivery of Fate* is based on her relationship with that Bryan guy, and don't want my dick associated with that asshole if I can help it. The last thing I need is her hearing his words from my lips when I'm trying to seduce her.

I choose *Vacation with the Enemy* and start chapter two since I already read the prologue at the VIP event and chapter one is in Daphne's point of view.

*"As I approach Daphne's front door, I'm overcome with a thousand anxious thoughts. I spent the last three weeks attempting to make amends and convince her that I'm not a bad guy. I lift my hand to knock but pause again. She doesn't want me the way I want her.*

*It's why I drove away that fuckface Zach. Daphne never forgave me for it.*

"*She opens the door with my hand still poised to rap on the door. She's fucking exquisite. Breathtaking. I'd give anything to be with this woman, if only she could move past the hurt I caused. No apology has ever sufficed.*"

This book has a different feel than *Delivery of Fate*, almost as if…

"Did he ever apologize?"

Becca frowns and I want to kiss the creases away. "Dylan? Yes. He did, but Daphne never forgave him." She chuckles. "I was in an alliteration phase there for a while. 'D' names kept popping up in my books."

I set my phone down and correct, "No, I meant Bryan. Did he ever apologize to you for fucking around with the other narrator?"

"Oh." Becca looks away, pausing for a moment. "No." It comes out just above a whisper.

"How could he do that to you?" I ask, mostly to myself, shaking my head in disbelief. "Fucking asshole." Her gaze lifts and, if she's still hurt by what he did, it isn't apparent on her face. Not like the night I read from *Delivery of Fate*. I take her hand and bring her knuckles to my lips. "His loss is my gain."

She offers a small smile and kisses my cheek. I turn and capture her mouth with mine, cupping her neck and pulling her closer. After spending the trip with her wrapped in my arms, not touching or kissing her isn't an option. She bites my lip as she pulls away. A groan escapes me. *How the fuck am I supposed to keep my hands to myself when I'm with her in public?*

"How are we supposed to work together when you kiss me like that, *my Julian?*" She says it in jest but I like too fucking much.

"I was thinking the exact same thing, *my Becca.*"

---

I dropped Becca off at her apartment an hour ago. Sitting on the couch in the living room of my suite, I can't focus. I'm working through a couple scenes, but every time I get to a scene with Bryan and Anna, it makes me sick to my stomach. I got an email this morning from the publisher that they are keeping Bryan, axing the name change to Julian. I know she did it to fuck with me when I started the project and I deserved it. The change back to Bryan is welcome.

The character's roles are reversed. Anna cheats on Bryan with his brother. As I'm reading through it, it's easy to tell what parts are drawn from experience. Anna ends up with Bryan's brother, where in real life, Bryan ends up with the other narrator. Becca was definitely hurting when she wrote this book.

As I skim the chapter, my eyes catch on the nickname "kitten." *Fuck, isn't that what Bryan called Becca at the restaurant?* This is worse than I thought. I need to pull myself from the project. At the very least, she can't be present while I'm recording.

I scroll my emails and create a new message.

**To**: Andre Stark

**From**: Julian Evans

**Subject**: Delivery of Fate by Merlot Bennet — Amendment to Contract

Andre,

Please remove the clause that Merlot has to be present for the recordings. Also, is there any way they would consider removing the fraternization policy?

Regards,

Julian

I close out of my email and tuck my phone in my back pocket. A minute or so later, it buzzes with an incoming call.

"Hey, Andre."

"Please tell me you're not fucking Merlot," Andre grits out.

"Of course not," I lie. I'd hardly call what we did "fucking," though...

"Bullshit. Why do you want me to request a change to your contract then? Fuck. It's the other narrator, isn't it? Merlot had the addition added to all of her contracts after everything that happened with her first and third books. She won't budge."

"It's not Caroline," I insist. "Look, if we can't change the fraternization policy, at least make it so Merlot doesn't have to be present while I'm recording. Her story... It's not just fiction. You know some of that shit happened to her."

"It's not your problem," he spits. "She wrote the book. If she didn't want to hear it recorded, she should've never published it. Everyone knows that her narrator, Bryan, was the inspiration for her novel. It's not your fault she named her character after him. It was sloppy on her part."

His comments feel very similar to "if she didn't want attention, she shouldn't have dressed like that," and my stomach churns. Victim blaming at its finest. I clench the phone tighter. I don't know the whole story, but I've put together that the entire literary world knows the asshole did some shady things and fucked over the infamous Merlot Bennet.

"I'll talk to Becca about it and see if we can get rid of it."

"No," he barks, "you're not going to talk to her about this. It's legal shit, Julian. Come on, you know better. What's this about?"

I blow out a long breath. "You're right. I just don't feel comfortable recording in front of her."

"I know. She's the biggest name you've done work for. I assure you, she's professional and I've heard nothing but good things about working with her. You'll be fine. The contract is iron clad since you're doing it pro-bono.

They wanted to protect themselves. Listen, I've gotta run, but if you need anything else, let me know."

*Fuck.*

"Okay, thanks."

We hang up and I stare at the wall in front of me. What started out as a chance to spend time with her is no longer a blessing, it's a fucking curse. I rake my hands through my hair. I need to talk to her about this. I pull up my contacts, emails, texts… *Scroll, scroll, scroll.* I don't have her number.

I've had my cock deep inside this woman, how the hell do I not have her number?

# 19

## BECCA

*They meet on ~~a plane~~ the subway and there's instant chemistry. He wants to see her again, so he goes behind her back and takes on her ~~audiobook~~ book cover to see her again.*

The words are flowing.

I haven't written this fast in… I don't know how long, if ever. I just need to get the outline on paper and I'll worry about writing and embellishing later.

*She's a ~~romance~~ ~~romcom~~ satire author. He is ~~a graphic designer~~ owns the largest design firm in the US.*

I knew he looked like a hot younger brother in a billionaire romance…

*He presses her against the building and kisses her in the rain.*

*He whisks her off to ~~St. Tropez~~ Italy because she's never been.*

*She falls in love with a man she's only known for a week.*

Fuck.

I slump back in my chair and toss my pencil onto my desk. Julian's only been in my life a week. *One week.* How can I fall for a man I barely know? He'll be gone in a few weeks. I don't know anything about him, other than what my search engine provided.

When's his birthday? I don't know. He feels like a Cancer, or maybe I'm just projecting a water sign on him because of St. Tropez.

What's his middle name? Probably George… George Glass. I snicker at my own *Brady Bunch* movie joke.

What's his favorite sport? Shit. Um… rugby? Maybe baseball?

Who did he vote for in the last election? Fuck. Do I even want to know?

Who's his favorite *Ted Lasso* character? Maybe Roy. No. Jamie. But it should be Roy. We'll totally fight about it.

I know nothing about Julian, other than how he makes me feel. And, fuck, he makes me feel good. I haven't talked to him since he dropped me off and it feels so strange to go from being in bed with someone, feeling all coupley, to radio silence.

Maybe he's just a rich player who just wanted to get in my pants? No. Who the hell flies someone to a whole other country just to fuck them? That's not a thing.

I rummage in my bag and take out my phone.

Do I call? Do I text? Do I email?

All at once, I realize I have nothing. Only a physical address for his winery in Temecula and… I know what hotel and room he's in! But I can't just show up, knock on his door and say "hey, I realized I know nothing about you, but I'm probably falling for you. Want to get to know each other before we *get to know each other?*"

Can I go see him?

No.

But what if I did?

Why, though? I know damn well I'd end up naked the moment I crossed the threshold. He basically singes my clothes to ashes with his eyes.

I groan and glance at my keys taunting me on my desk. Why do I want to get to know him? He's leaving.

Maybe we can grab a coffee? Nope, I'll end up naked.

A drink? Super naked. What is super naked? I don't know, but I fucking want it. Right now.

I head to the kitchen and reach above my fridge, pulling out a bottle of blue label whiskey. It's not my first choice but I've read and written enough strong female characters to know that this choice could be the answer to my predicament.

I grab a glass from my cabinet and a few ice cubes, then pour two fingers. I raise the glass to my lips, but only taste the whiskey for a moment when there's a knock at my door.

*Julian?*

After setting down my glass, I cautiously make my way to the door. When I reach it, I dust off my pants, push my hair behind my shoulders, and straighten my posture. I open the door.

"Hey… Mrs. Goldstein." My face falls as soon as I realize it's not *him*. Why would it be? You don't just show up at someone's apartment. That only happens in books.

"Hi, dear. I was wondering if I could trouble you for a moment?"

I blow out a sigh of relief. As much as I wanted it to be Julian, I'm glad for the distraction. "Of course. How can I help?"

"Daddy is stuck under the bed."

This sweet seventy-something woman just asked me to help her with her… Daddy.

"Sure, I can help you with *Daddy*." I try my hardest not to laugh. I've heard her through my walls recently saying things like, "No, bad Daddy." How the fuck did a grown ass man end up under a bed? But good for them for adding a bit of kink at their age.

"Thank you, sweetheart. I hope he doesn't give you any trouble. He can scratch."

My eyes widen. I shouldn't judge. I can only hope that, when I'm this old, I live such a rich sex life. "Sure, lead the way."

I close my door and follow her to her apartment. When I enter, this looks like something out of Dolores Umbridge's office. Props to Daddy for being cool with it.

Cautiously, I head into the bedroom. "Okay, so how did…" My voice trails off as I realize there's no man under the bed. "So… how can I help?" Please tell me this isn't some sort of imaginary man situation. Dementia?

"Under the bed," she insists.

I crouch down to search for an imaginary hot old man my neighbor made up.

*Meow.*

I laugh so hard my stomach hurts. "Come on, *Daddy*. Come here." I pat my lap. He comes immediately and jumps up onto the bed. "Well, looks like Daddy is good to go." I can't help the chuckle that escapes me when I say his name.

"Thank you, Becca. Daddy just wasn't listening to me. He was being a damn brat, if you ask me."

I bite my lip to keep from laughing harder. "No problem. I'll head back but let me know if Daddy gets stuck again, okay?"

She nods and I exit her apartment in giggles as soon as she is out of earshot. I shake my head and as my gaze lifts to my door, there's a man with his hand poised to knock. He looks to me and...

"Julian."

## 20

---

## JULIAN

"Julian," she breathes.

"My Becca." It takes everything in me not to touch her. I know I shouldn't be here. I just couldn't stay away.

Neither one of us move for several seconds. My chest rises and falls, twice. I watch Becca suck in a shaky breath.

As if something feral unleashes within me, I close the distance, take her face in my hands, and bring her lips to mine.

This isn't the kiss in the rain.

This isn't St. Tropez.

This transcends everything I knew about kissing a woman.

"What are you doing here?" she asks against my lips after we lost ourselves in each other for a moment.

"I didn't have your number." I reluctantly break our kiss. I search her eyes. *Does she want me here?* Her expression is unreadable, so I immediately apologize, "I'm sorry, I know I shouldn't have just stopped by. I just—"

Becca hooks her hand behind my neck and pulls me back to her, our mouths crashing together. My heart ached not being with her. Fuck, this is ridiculous. How does she have this sort of impact on me? We hardly know one another.

"Don't apologize," she says between kisses.

"I missed you." The words tumble from me before I can give them a second thought.

The door to her neighbor's apartment opens and we both pull back abruptly. "Becca, so sorry to bother you again, but... oh. Who is this handsome man?" the older woman asks.

Becca looks at me. "He's, uh... my *friend*."

I'm sure as fuck not her friend. These brief moments she's not kissing me, I feel like I can't breathe—as if I need her more than oxygen. No *friend* could have that kind of effect on me.

"Oh pish posh. You two were sucking face in the hallway. Do you think I was born yesterday?"

I cough to cover up a laugh. "My apologies."

"You were going to say you needed something. How can I help?" Becca asks.

"I was just going to see if you could make sure Daddy gets dinner tonight. He seems to like you. I'm headed out and he'll be a real asshole when I return if he doesn't eat."

*Daddy?*

Becca chuckles. "Sure thing. Anything else?"

"Yes." The older woman eyes me curiously, then addresses Becca, "If this one isn't yours, can I have him?"

"I love a cougar as much as the next man, but I'm taken." I nod my head in Becca's direction. When I glance over, Becca's blushing.

"The good ones always are." The woman pats me on the shoulder as she passes us to leave. "Don't forget about Daddy!" she hollers, making her way down the stairs. "If he gives you any trouble, a quick swat on the ass does the trick."

Becca smirks and once the woman is out of earshot, she asks, "Taken, huh?"

Guiding her until her back is pressed against the wall, I lean over her and brace myself with my hand above her head. "Yeah, I'd say so." I brush a kiss to her neck and she lets out a sigh that quickly turns into a moan. Fuck. I love that I can do that to her.

"Let me grab my purse. We can head out," she says breathlessly.

I groan against her shoulder. "I thought you didn't want to be seen together."

"You can keep your hands to yourself for a few hours."

"Doubtful." I nip at her earlobe, which causes her to swallow hard.

Becca places her hands on my chest and gently pushes me away so she can head into her apartment. I wait at the doorway, itching to touch her, but remain leaning against the frame while she grabs her things.

I feel like I've been waiting my entire life to meet someone like her—someone who makes our conversations feel like an exciting chess match. She's vivacious, so full of fire. One taste of her and I've developed a bit of an obsession.

"Are you okay?"

I blink away my thoughts. "Yeah, why?"

"You were frowning. Kind of an international sign for something being wrong." She swipes her thumb between my brows and her simple touch has my face relaxed into a more neutral expression. "There. That's better. Can't be seen in public with a grouch. What would the tabloids say?" She playfully nudges me backward so she can close the door and lock it.

"Where are we headed?" I take her hand and kiss the back of it. "I need to give my driver a heads up."

"Driver? No, we're calling a rideshare or walking. I've already been spoiled enough by your lavish but incredibly magical trip."

I chuckle. "I hired him earlier today. He'll be my driver until I leave New York." *Which might be never.* "No need for a rideshare or taxi."

"Okay, fancypants. I accept your ride, but I'm buying the drinks."

*Not a chance.*

"Or, you can just let me take you out on a date, like a normal couple," I counter.

She raises a curious eyebrow. "Now we're a couple?"

I close the distance and tuck her hair behind her ear as I lean in with a low voice, in hopes of seducing my beautiful stranger. "You want to be mine as much as I want to be yours, my Becca." When I pull back, her cheeks are flushed and eyes wide. *Fucking perfect.* "You can pick the place, but" —I take her chin between my thumb and forefinger and kiss her softly—"I'm treating my girl to a real date tonight."

---

"I'll have two Manhattans, please." The bartender nods and dives right into making our drinks.

Becca chose a jazz club four blocks from her house so that we could A) walk here and B) she could ensure we wouldn't end up naked. Since it's dark, I can still touch her. Hold her hand. Whisper to her how much I want her.

I do none of these.

I reign in my temptation and focus on the music as soon as I return to the table with our drinks. This game of cat and mouse we're playing is torture—as if she wants me to test her. She places her hand on my thigh, entirely too close to where I desperately want her. A quick unzip and she'd have the freedom to touch me.

If anyone were to ask me, what my intentions are when this audiobook is done, my answer would be simple: Becca. I'd give up every dime to my name for just one day with this woman. We already missed out on sight-seeing in St. Tropez because my cock had other plans. If I want to play this right, I need to keep it in my pants.

The trumpet blares with a solo, but I can't enjoy it. Becca's hand wanders lower between my legs, her pinky grazing my balls. Fuck. I take her hand in mine, inter-lacing our fingers, squeezing tight. She groans. I'm not about to give in to her sexy as fuck game she's playing.

I softly kiss her neck and insist, "Keep that up and I'll have a car here in less than four minutes to take you home. Be my good girl and keep your hands to yourself or expect my own hand between your legs."

Becca bites her lip, as if this is a dare. "When have I ever been a good girl?"

"Fuck," I mutter.

"When's your birthday?"

Her question takes me by surprise. "July 19th. Why?"

She chuckles. "I knew you were a Cancer, but not *exactly* six months from mine."

It dawns on me that I have no fucking clue how old she is. So, I ask.

"I'm 33. You?"

"24." I try to keep a serious face but fail immediately. "36."

She lets out a sigh of relief and a short laugh. "I mean, you look young but not *that* young. Okay, so what's your middle name?"

"*Shh.* What is this? Twenty questions? We came here to enjoy the music." I have no issue telling her but I want to watch her squirm. Becca's obviously on a mission for information and I intend to draw it out as long as possible. She'll win this round, but in the end, I'll be the real winner.

Becca shifts uncomfortably in her seat, as expected, but she looks down slightly. "Sorry," she whispers.

Fuck. She must've taken me seriously. Just like me, she's looking for answers. I should've just told her instead of playing hard to get.

I lift her chin and kiss her harder than I should dare to do in public, hoping she won't stop me. "James," I say against her lips. I reluctantly break our kiss, pulling back but still sharing a breath. "My parents wanted me to be J.J. but it never stuck." Her eyes dart between mine. "But turn away from me like that again, and expect to be punished for it—I won't let you come as I taste that delicious cunt of yours." She bites her lip and it takes everything in me to not drop to my knees and worship her right here. "You want to know something? Ask it. I'm an open book."

## 21

---

## BECCA

This all feels like a game—one I'm losing. I'm torn between wanting to get to know him and shielding my heart from the inevitable pain that's to come when this is over. Against my better judgment, I resign myself to the fact that this is a once in a lifetime love... *lust*. Once in a lifetime *lust*. I'd be foolish to not give in to whatever this is.

*Maybe he wasn't joking about moving here? What if he moved here and it didn't work out? I'd feel like a real bitch if he moved across the country and things didn't end in a happily ever after. Why am I even considering this? I've known him a fucking week...*

"You're notorious for non-answers, my Becca, but I'll ask anyway. What's yours?"

"My what?" I'm so lost in thought that I've completely forgotten what we were talking about.

"Your middle name. Unless you want to give me the

infamous name of your…" Julian glances to my lap and back up again.

The music stops and there's clapping all around us but I don't break eye contact with Julian. I contemplate not telling him either name, keeping the mystery alive.

The air is thick between us. My heart rate has slowed and it's as if time has stopped altogether. The flame from the candle on the table casts shadows on his face, the flecks of gold shimmering in his eyes as the firelight dances across them.

A cocktail waitress approaches the table. "Pardon me. Can I grab you two something to drink."

Julian's eyes never leave mine as he reaches into his pocket, pulling out a few bills. He glances at her long enough to say, "Two Manhattans, please. Keep the change." He hands her the cash. I sneak a glance and it's two $100 bills. His gaze returns to mine as she walks away. "You're really not going to tell me, are you?"

I swallow hard. "Marie." I clarify, "My *middle* name is Marie."

He leans in to kiss my neck, and whispers, "I suppose I don't need the name of your pussy. The only thing I intend to ever call it is *mine*."

My breath catches. "Um, well, *someone's* been reading romance books. You have the growly book boyfriend thing down."

"I'm not fictional. But I wouldn't mind being…" He sits back and takes a drink, setting down the now-empty glass.

"Mind being what?"

"Since you're a romance author, I would've assumed you'd be able to pick up on a man flirting with you. *Your boyfriend*, Becca. I wouldn't mind being your *boyfriend*." A boyish grin spreads across his face.

"Are you going to give me your letterman's jacket too? Or your class ring? Are we courting, *my Julian?*"

Julian laughs, biting his lip. "Baby, I'd give you whatever you want, if you were mine. I'm sure I could go back home and rummage in the basement of my parents' house to find my old jacket. I was captain of the football team, you know. You'd be the talk of the whole school wearing it." He shrugs off his jacket and places it around my shoulders. "This will have to do for now."

The waitress returns with our drinks. I take a sip of mine and say into my glass, "You said *if* I was yours. Sounds to me like it's undecided."

He takes my glass and sets it on the table. "It's for you to decide. For the next few weeks while we're recording, I'll keep my distance. Flirting aside, I like you. *A lot*. So, you better believe as soon as we're done, I want to date you and, dare I say, *be with you*. But you get to decide what you want here."

*I want you.*

Whatever this is going on between us, it's feeling dangerously close to a serious relationship. For the first time all week, I'm actually okay with it.

"Daddy's a cat?" Julian tries to contain his laughter

"What? You thought he was some sexy old man? It's okay, I thought so too."

I open the can of cat food and it smells horrid. I quickly scoop it into a bowl for Daddy so we can get the hell out of here. The last thing I want is for it to permeate my clothes.

I lock up Mrs. Goldstein's place and walk down the hall to mine. I pause with the key in the lock, but I don't turn. "Would you, um, like to come inside?" I ask, my gaze fixed on the handle.

"Yes, but…" Julian's pause has me looking up, my eyes searching his. He was waiting for it. "I would rather take you out tomorrow night. Would you go out with me, my Becca?"

"Maybe."

His eyebrows raise. "Maybe?"

"Yeah. Maybe," I confirm. "If you can pick somewhere we won't get caught."

He cages me in with his hand, propping himself up against the door behind me. "If I promise, is that a yes?"

I swallow hard. My voice nearly cracking, I reply, "Yes."

Julian closes the distance and kisses me softly. It's warm, sweet, and gentle… a first date kiss. I laugh lightly at the thought.

"Is there something funny?" He pulls back an inch. I whimper at the loss of contact.

"Oh, no. I was just thinking that we technically had a first date. Kind of backwards, don't you think?"

"Only a little. I knew the moment I met you that this would be anything but normal." He presses a chaste kiss to my cheek. "Goodnight, my Becca. I'll see you tomorrow."

Julian pushes off the door and steps away to head downstairs. "Wait." He turns back. "You forgot something."

"I'm not coming inside. As much as I'd love to have your naked body wrapped up in mine, I have to prepare for tomorrow. Big day recording a book by the sexiest woman I've ever known," he says with a wink.

"No, I mean yes, I want you to stay with me. But you forgot to ask for my number." I can't help the grin on my face.

He shakes his head, amused. "You're absolutely right." He hands me his phone and I put my name and number in his contacts.

"There. Now there's no reason for you to pop by unannounced." I hand it back to him.

"Sorry about that."

"No, you're not... but neither am I."

# 22

## JULIAN

Beads of sweat collect on my forehead and I run my sweaty palms over my pants. I've never been so nervous. I'd rather be in a spelling bee naked than narrate this book in front of her. When I did it before, it was in the comfort of my hotel room, where I could control everything. Also, I was trying to seduce her... and it epically backfired.

They placed us in a small recording space, since it's just the two of us. "When I start, you'll need to not move or make any sudden noises or I'll have to re-record it."

Becca lets out a soft laugh and nods. "Okay."

I set everything up and begin. "*Chapter Two. Bryan.*" I click my clicker twice to indicate the end of narration for the female narrator to take over. "*No one has to know, kitten...*"

I pull off my headphones after four paragraphs. Bile rises in my throat at the thought of him being with her. I'm not sure where her story ends and fiction begins. I know this is a role reversal, where Anna is the one who cheats on Bryan, but the fact that he was with her in the first place… I want to punch a wall.

"What's wrong?" Becca genuinely asks. "That sounded great."

I tilt my head to crack my neck. "I just need a little break."

"Break? You've only narrated a few paragraphs." She looks at the equipment. "Is the recording off?"

I nod, unable to look at her for fear that I'd do something reckless and steal her away from here and never look back. I had no idea I'd be walking into this when I took on the book. I just wanted to spend time with her.

I *am* spending time with her, I remind myself. Without this book, I wouldn't be with the most fascinating woman I've ever met. I know we haven't slapped a label on whatever this is between us, but I'm hers in every sense of the word.

"Julian," she sighs. "Was this a bad idea?"

*Yes.*

"No. Of course not. I just… Why did you name your character Bryan?"

The question takes her by surprise, warranting a few moments to reply. "I was writing my way out of a break up. My agent said to keep it in, so I did. I didn't expect *Delivery of Fate* to take off. Who the fuck wants to read about a woman who cheats on her boss with his brother?" She shakes her head. "Can we please just get through this?"

"No, baby, I can't do this. Not with you here."

Her eyes wide, she glances again at my switchboard. "Julian—"

"It's not on," I assure her. "Come here." Becca freezes, her eyes wide. I roll my office chair so I'm facing her. Her breathing is heavy in anticipation. I cup her cheek and kiss her. "I'm sorry," I mutter against her lips before pulling back. "I don't want you here when I have to get into character, calling Anna 'kitten' or when I have to say things from his point of view… as *him*."

"You're not him," she says softly. "The story is fiction."

"When he tells her that she's his good girl and tells her to drop to her knees? That was fiction?"

Becca wets her lips. "He never said that to me. Tonight, I'll go through the notes and highlight things that were real. I promise that wasn't one of them; he never called me that. So, if you want me on my knees for you, you better not be walking on eggshells when you ask."

My cock twitches in my pants. I ask for a compromise. "I won't record in front of you, but I'll do edits with you."

"One condition."

"Okay?" I eye her suspiciously.

"During the on-page sex scenes, will you do them live?"

"Fuck no," I blurt out.

Becca leans in to press a soft kiss to my lips. It's sweet but also sexy as fuck. She knows she has me wrapped around her finger. "Those scenes were completely fictional," she insists. "When you're moaning, I want it to be real."

"I'll be moaning someone else's name. I have no desire to call out 'Anna' as I come." She reaches between my legs and rubs her palm across my length, making me groan.

"Fuck it. Get over here." I pull her onto me and she giggles in response. I don't care if she dry humps me, I need to feel her body against mine. I want to claim her, own her.

"I doubt you'll get any work done this way. I should go." She pretends to get up but I keep her firmly rooted in place, gripping her hips. "*Fine,* I guess I'll stay. Hot, broody man requires my assistance. Who am I to say no?"

"I sure as hell could never say no to you. What do you want, my Becca? Ask and it's yours."

"That's a lot of power to give someone." Becca bites her lip and grinds herself onto me.

"I'll make you a deal." I kiss her neck, lightly nipping as I pull away. She leans into my touch, making it incredibly difficult to focus on, well, anything. "You get your sexy ass out of here. I'll record a few chapters, and when I'm finished, I'll take you out on the date I was promised."

"Counter offer." She takes off her shirt, revealing a lacy dark green bra. "You touch me. Right now."

"Oh, my sweet Becca, if I touched you, we wouldn't leave here until well after hours. I'm not going to start something I can't finish." I pull down the top of her bra and take one of her nipples into my mouth; teasing, licking, sucking. She leans into me, arching her back. "Tasting you, on the other hand, is something else entirely."

My phone vibrates on the table. I'm normally careful to keep it on silent but have been too distracted by her to keep with routine. It breaks the sexy spell she has me under and I reluctantly pull the cups of her bra back up and over her perfect fucking tits.

"You're mine, my Becca. The minute I'm done recording, I intend to pick up *exactly* where I left off."

She exhales slowly. "All right, *my Julian.* You win, but it better be worth the wait."

I grip the front of her neck and pull her lips to mine. She moans into my mouth as I own this piece of her.

*Mine.*

"Baby, you have no idea what I'm capable of. In six hours, I'm coming by your place. I want you naked and spread wide for me on your bed so I can feast on you until you can't take it anymore. So help me, if that sweet old woman knocks on your door asking you to keep it down, I'll have her rethinking the name of that cat of hers."

Becca's infectious laugh fills the studio. "I thought I was going to be taken out on a date tonight, not bringing home a Dom. And I'm not calling you Daddy."

"We are absolutely going out tonight; I'm a man of my word. You, my beautiful stranger, are going to come all over my face before we leave, though."

# 23

## JULIAN

Recording without her present is the only way I'll be able to get through the book. Every time Bryan called Anna kitten, I had to stop recording—my jaw would tick and the lines were coming out gritty. I know she wanted a commanding voice for this character, but the unadulterated anger I felt coursing through my veins wasn't quite the same thing.

I got through a few chapters after she left. Now that I'm done for the day, all I want is to drive over to her place and claim her as mine. One week was all it took for her to turn me into some sort of possessive fae prince in a fantasy book.

Becca's not expecting me for a few hours and I have a bit of work to do. The drive to the hotel is quiet, so I take out my phone, which is still on silent from recording, and switch it over to regular volume. There's a few hundred emails but only four text messages—all four from *her*. I can't help the smile that crosses my face the moment I see her name.

MY BECCA

Not sure where we're going tonight, but
will this do?

It's followed by a photo of her in an all black dress with
a low v-cut neckline that makes me want to trace the
outline with my tongue.

Or this?

I'm hard the minute I see the next photo. My slacks are
now entirely too tight, I have to adjust myself. She's on
the bed, naked and covered by a thin white sheet. It
hugs her incredible curves and…

"Damon, change of plans. Take me to Becca's."

My driver looks in the rearview mirror and asks, "The
one on the Upper East Side from yesterday?"

"That's the one."

Damon nods and we make our way to her apartment.
Thankfully, it's only a twenty minute drive, but it's also
the longest twenty minutes of my life. The pull I have
towards this woman is fucking intense.

When I was here yesterday, a man was entering the
building and let me in. Today, I'm not as lucky. I press
the intercom button for apartment 17 to call her.

"Hello."

"Good evening, my Becca." I keep my voice low and
purposefully seductive.

"You're early." The door beeps to unlock. "Come on up."

I take the stairs two at a time. When I finally reach her door, I blow out a deep breath and knock three times.

"It's open," she yells, muffled through the door.

When I open the door, I find her cross-legged on her couch, with her laptop perched on her lap. She's wearing a pair of black leggings and oversized NYU sweatshirt that has seen better days, but she's still fucking stunning. Her hair is tied up in a messy bun and she has her purple rimmed glasses on. I haven't seen her wear them since the plane and it gives me flashbacks to meeting her for the first time, when my life changed forever.

Becca doesn't look up from her laptop. "Five more minutes." I sit down on the couch next to her, kissing her on the cheek. She hums in response. "You're early."

"So I've been told." I try to take a peek at her work but she shuts the laptop as soon as she realizes what I'm doing. "Care to share?"

"It's not ready. I... I'm working on something new." Becca's cheeks are now dusted dark pink.

"Must be quite the steamy scene you're working on. You're flushed." I move a rogue strand of hair out of her face and tuck it behind her ear. "When can I read it? Or I can act it out for you." I move to kneel in front of her, carefully taking off her glasses and setting them on the coffee table behind me. I remove the laptop from her lap and set it aside. "I thought I told you to be naked when I arrived."

Becca removes her sweatshirt, tossing it to the ground, revealing she was wearing nothing underneath. *Fuck.* "You were early. I had work to get done." She uncrosses her legs, placing one on either side of me as she slips off her leggings... without underwear. "Why are you still dressed?"

I pull her legs, forcing her closer to me. "Because I'm not going to fuck you... I just missed the taste of you." I don't have condoms with me, otherwise I'd be deep inside her. Right fucking now. I lick slowly up her beautiful cunt and swirl my tongue around her clit, making her shudder.

"You can't just keep... *ahhh*... going down on me, Julian."

I chuckle against her and, between licks, reply, "This pussy is mine. I can do whatever I like with it." Her head falls back as she lets out a soft moan. "That's right, baby. Let me make you feel good." I press two fingers inside her and curl them at the same pace as my tongue.

"Oh, fuck!" she cries out and I add a third.

Hearing her sexy moans has me fantasizing about waking up every morning with her—getting her wet and ready with my fingers before I drive into her bare. I allow myself to live in the daydream for a moment. She's close to coming for me, tightening around my fingers as I suck hard on her clit, nearly sending her over the edge.

"*Julian.*" My name comes out as a plea.

"Yes, baby?"

"Right there. Don't st…" She comes hard and fast for me. Fuck dinner. I'd gladly feast on her all night if it meant I'd get to hear my name spill from her lips over and over again.

I kiss the inside of her thigh, looking up at her through my lashes as I carefully remove my fingers from her pussy, sucking them clean. She grips my shirt, pulling me to her. Our lips are less than an inch apart. Her breath is labored and I steal it for myself, kissing her hard. She wraps her arms around me as if she can't get close enough.

"Are you ready to head out?" I ask against her lips.

She chuckles and pulls back. "Does it look like I'm ready?" I glance down at her beautiful naked body, biting my lip. "I was promised a date, but if you want to do other things, I'm not opposed."

"No," I groan. "We already missed out on seeing St. Tropez because I was inside you the entire time. You're not missing out on what I have planned, no matter how much I want that *lady garden* of yours wrapped around my cock."

Her head hangs back in laughter and I can't help myself as I kiss her exposed neck. I refrain from leaving a mark like a fucking vampire, as much as I want to claim her. I've waited my whole life for a woman like Becca, and it's fucking irrational that I'm feeling this way, but I want her to be…

*Mine.*

She cups each side of my face, kissing me once, then gets up without a word and walks toward her bedroom to get dressed.

Pausing at the door, she turns back. "Oh, you might want to rein in the whole growling *mine* against my neck. Unless you plan on following through on that."

*Fuck. I'm falling in love with her.*

## 24

---

## BECCA

I'm wound up so damn tight. About an hour before Julian showed up, there was a delivery from a courier containing a giant dress box with a note saying simply "Wear me. -J." As if he wasn't spoiling me enough with selfless orgasms, he buys me yet another extravagant gift.

I slip into the emerald green, floor-length silk dress that makes my ass look amazing and trumpets at the bottom. It's low-cut and my boobs are practically spilling out of it. It leaves little to the imagination—it may as well be painted on. Staring at myself in my full length mirror, I swipe my hand down my body at non-existent wrinkles. My gaze lifts as I spot Julian approaching. We lock eyes in the mirror briefly before his arm wraps around me from behind. My favorite move of his.

*Can I have a favorite move? We've known each other for, what, eight seconds?*

Julian kisses my neck and whispers, "You look incredible."

"A fancy dress will do that." I turn in his hold, placing my hands on his chest. "You didn't need to buy me anything, I could've worn the black one."

"The green one matches your eyes... among other things," he says, biting his lip.

"Where are we going that I'd need something this... naked?"

He chuckles and brushes his nose against mine, practically begging me to kiss him. "Can't I just buy you something pretty and enjoy how fucking amazing it looks on you?"

"As long as your reasons are completely selfish, I'll let it slide." I close the short distance, only offering a ghost of a kiss. He groans in response and pulls my body closer to him. "Where are we going?"

"When was the last time you saw a Broadway show?"

---

"This isn't Broadway, Julian. This is *Hamilton*... orchestra seating." I don't need to research it to know these seats are incredibly expensive, especially since we have backstage passes to meet the cast after the show.

Julian rests his arm behind me and whispers beside my ear, his breath tickling my neck, "Only the best for my girl." While he says it playfully, my stomach flips at the implication that I'm his.

He's not wrong. I know things have moved fast between us, but I've never felt this way about someone before.

Since the moment we met, I've felt a connection with him, like we are old souls that found each other after years apart.

"It's too much, but… thank you." I kiss his cheek and his sweet smile spreads from ear to ear.

Lights flash, indicating the show's about to start. I sit back in my seat and his thumb swipes slowly back and forth on my shoulder. I lean into his touch. We shouldn't see anyone we know here, but if we did, his touch is innocent enough that I could say we're just friends and I'm cold.

Ok, that's a lie. All of this is incredibly compromising, but I enjoy his touch so much that I really don't care who sees his arm around me.

I've watched the show so many times on streaming services, I can recite the entire thing from memory. Song after song, I'm biting my tongue to not belt out the lyrics. When the final song before intermission ends, we give a standing ovation. Julian's hand wanders down my back, squeezing my hip once before he begins his own applause. The simple touch gives me butterflies.

"Let's stretch our legs; it's a three hour show." He offers his hand and I debate taking it, but I know he can sense my hesitation. I take a deep breath and place my hand in his. Bringing our joined hands up to his lips, he asks softly, "What are you doing to me, my Becca?"

"I don't know," I reply honestly. The world around me doesn't exist. In this moment, it's just Julian.

I search for his trademark gold flecks in his irises, not finding them. His hungry eyes are almost completely black as he stares back at me.

A woman clears her throat behind me, forcing my gaze from Julian to her as she attempts to move past us. When it returns to him, he slides his free hand into my hair and kisses me. I let him, even if it's a risk. As he tries to take it further and dip his tongue into my mouth, I become acutely aware of how this looks and pull back.

"Not here," I whisper.

He chuckles, shaking his head. "I'm sorry. I'm a grown man trying to grope you here in the middle of a theater." He takes a deep breath. "I can't *not* touch you. I can't explain it."

"Come on. I have an idea." I bite my lip and take his hand, guiding him down the aisle. I feel like a damn teenager trying to skip class; I'm half tempted to pull him into a secluded bathroom or dark corner. I'm ready to go home and make love… *have sex* with this beautiful man.

When we reach the main lobby, it dawns on me that he was able to secure these tickets fairly quickly, but on the plane he asked me for museum recommendations. He also seems to know this theater like the back of his hand. *This isn't his first time here.* I pause and look up at him, my eyes searching his. "How often do you come to New York?"

"About once a month. Why?"

I can't help the chuckle that escapes me. "Then, why did you need museum recommendations?" His smile gives him away. "You're such a flirt."

"I would have talked to you about the weather or even your favorite, boring as hell, non-fiction book, if it meant I had your attention for two minutes. Becca, I should tell you—"

"Well, isn't this a pleasant surprise."

I don't know who this man is, but Julian pulls away from me immediately.

"Andre. Good to see you. May I introduce Merlot Bennet? Merlot, this is Andre, my agent."

*Shit. This is a bookish thing.*

"Ah, the infamous Merlot." Andre offers his hand and I take it. He presses a gross as fuck kiss to my knuckles, his wiry beard scratching my skin. "Pleasure is mine."

"Nice to meet you." The moment my hand is free, I discreetly brush it against Julian's coat, not wanting any potential saliva on my dress. "I was just telling Julian I'm not feeling well and need to head home. I apologize for not being able to stay and socialize." I look at Julian, his hurt apparent on his face as I back away. "Thank you for an unforgettable evening, and Andre, it was so great to meet the man Julian has said nothing but wonderful things about. Excuse me."

I step away before things become even more awkward. The fact that I can't openly be with Julian is shattering my heart into thousands of pieces, now more than ever.

I'm falling for a man that I can't have… at least not right now.

# 25

# JULIAN

"You're a *fucking* idiot. You're sleeping with Merlot, aren't you?"

"That's none of your business," I grit out. I was careless when I asked about the contract, but Andre won't say anything that would compromise his commission. *Right?*

"You're in breach of contract. That's absolutely my business," Andre huffs.

I rake a hand through my hair. "I need to go. We'll talk about this another time."

Andre shakes his head in disappointment and I walk away in search of Becca. Exiting the double doors, I find her waiting out front, typing on her phone. She's a vision, even with a scowl on her face.

"There you are."

She looks up from her phone. "Here I am."

"Come on, let's head back in. Intermission is almost over and they'll lock us out if we aren't in our seats." I take her hand but she pulls it back. "Don't worry about Andre."

"It isn't just Andre. We're being careless… *I'm* being careless. If we get caught, it would be a PR nightmare. This might just be some sort of hobby for you, but writing is what pays the bills for me. I can't afford bad press around this audiobook, especially with my new novel coming out in a few months." She takes a deep breath. "I'm sorry. I should go."

Becca looks away but I guide her by the chin to look back at me. "No."

"No, what?"

"No to all of it. This isn't just a hobby for me. I might not need the money, but this is my job and reputation that you're belittling. I take pride in my work."

"I'm sorry. I shouldn't have said—"

"I'm not finished." I slide my hand along her jaw and tangle it into her hair, swiping my thumb on her cheek. "I promise I won't let anything happen to your books," I say softly. "But I have no intention of ending whatever this is between us. You want to keep things quiet, I get it. Consider this our last outing until the audiobook is finished and I'm no longer under contract." I rest my forehead on hers. "In case I'm not making myself clear, I want *you*, my Becca. So, we'll be careful and I'll play by your rules."

"This doesn't look innocent." Her voice comes out strangled.

I chuckle and pull her closer. "You're right."

"Julian," she whispers. "What the hell is this?" She pulls back an inch; her eyes dart between mine. "I want you. I want you more than I've wanted anyone in my life... None of this makes sense."

I bring her lips to mine. Her kisses are gentle, cautious, but still hold the same fire I crave from her.

None of the epic romances got it right. What I feel for Becca is deeper than anything Shakespeare could have came up with. Jane Austen's Darcy isn't even close. Maybe that guy from *Bridgerton* who burns for her, but even then... it's not enough. This woman in my arms completes me in a way I never thought possible. I've been hers from the moment I saw her.

A few raindrops hit the back of my head and I slowly step away from her. "Come back inside with me?" I ask hopefully.

"That was... did you just try to make love to my mouth?"

I can't help but laugh. "Are you sure you aren't a romcom author?" I kiss her cheek and, instead of taking her hand, I offer her my arm. "Shall we?"

We head inside to enjoy the rest of the show. I keep my hands to myself... sort of. Some part of my body's in contact with her at all times. Once it's over, we head backstage to meet the cast. They're all so incredibly kind and welcoming, even offering us a tour.

"Here's where some of the props are kept and…" The woman presses her fingers to her headset. "Sorry, I have to run and grab this. Feel free to look around. When you're done, Linda will meet you out front and can get you any autographed swag you want."

She walks away and, after spending the last couple hours in the dark next to her, my palm itches to touch Becca. She looks up into the rafters as she asks, "When was the last time you had a book-worthy moment, Julian?" When her gaze returns to mine, she offers a sly smile, biting her lip.

I take a step toward her. "I suppose it depends on the book."

"How about a spicy romance about an audiobook narrator who finds himself quite taken with a romance author? One where she can't stay away from him, no matter how hard she tries."

Becca closes the distance, leaving mere inches between us, still not touching me. She lifts her chin, a silent request for me to kiss her. I resist. Keeping her voice low, she adds, "Or maybe it's more of an erotica, where she drops to her knees for him whenever he asks."

*Fuck.*

I unconsciously lick my lips. "Yet, the heroine insists that she can't be seen in public with him."

"I don't see any *public* here. Ask me, Julian."

"I don't want you on your knees, baby." I turn her around, hold her by her throat against me, and kiss her bare shoulder. She lets out a breathy moan. "I want to bend you over and fuck you hard and fast, until you come all over my cock. I want my cum dripping down your leg as we walk out of here."

She swallows hard and I feel it in my hand. "It'll stain my dress." Her voice is just above a whisper.

"Good." I pull her impossibly closer, her ass pressed against my increasingly hard cock. "What do you want, my Becca?"

"You."

The simple word unleashes everything. I double check my surroundings. "Hands on the wall, baby." I crouch down to lift her dress up and around her waist. She's not wearing underwear. *Fuck*. I reach between her legs; she's already wet for me.

Reality sets in… I forgot condoms. How the fuck was I supposed to know I'd have an opportunity to fuck her at a Broadway show? I didn't get tickets for "Fucking at *Funny Girl*" or "Humping at *Hairspray*."

She must sense my hesitation, because she asks, "Everything okay back there?"

"Yeah." I reach around and drive two fingers inside her. She gasps and hangs her head back. "You're fucking perfect. There just isn't enough time to do what I want to with this pretty pussy of yours," I lie. My thumb plays with her clit as I keep up a punishing pace. "Are you going to be my good girl and come for me?"

"Yes," she whimpers.

"I need to take you home to fuck you properly." I pull my fingers out and suck them clean before turning her around and pressing her back against the wall. "We don't need to mess up this pretty dress of yours. I'll clean up every drop." I fall to my knees and without any warning, my mouth is on her clit. She grips my hair, pulling me closer and grinding against me.

"I need just a little—" I don't let her finish the sentence, I push my fingers into her cunt again, curling and teasing her. Time isn't on our side; I suck hard, knowing it will send her over the edge quickly. "Oh, right there, I'm going to—" My free hand covers her mouth as she comes for me. She sighs against my hand, making me chuckle against her pussy. It prolongs her orgasm and she clenches around my fingers. I remove them, bringing them to my mouth, and sucking them clean. I can't get enough of her.

"Attagirl." I lap up all of her before pulling her dress down. "What do you say we get out of here?"

She nods excitedly as I rise to my feet. "Yes," she breathes.

I'm about to kiss her when a stage hand approaches, startled when they find us. "Oh, sorry. I thought no one was back here. Did you two get lost?"

Becca clears her throat. "Yes, sorry. We were told to find…"

"Linda," I finish.

"Right this way." They guide us out of the theater to the front to meet Linda, who promised merchandise when I paid way too much for these last minute tickets. I almost insisted it was fine, but who am I to say no when Becca might want something?

"Hi, you must be Julian." Linda offers her hand. I keep my hand in my pocket since it was just inside my girl. "You'll have to excuse me. I need to use the restroom. Please, give her whatever she wants, no matter the cost." I kiss Becca's cheek and head to the bathroom.

I lean on the bathroom counter. I'm hard as hell and need to think about the unsexiest things I can think of...

Nothing comes to mind. All I can think about is *her*.

I wash my hands, blow out a deep breath, and resign myself to the fact that I'll need to keep my dick in my pants for the next half hour, at least.

I head back to find Becca laughing with Linda. I only catch the last part of whatever Becca is saying. "He definitely is... Oh, hey, ready to head out."

"Yeah, you?"

She lifts a bag with a wide smile. "Some of it was signed by Lin himself! Let's go home and I'll show you everything."

*Home.*

I take Becca's hand. With no one around, she lets me without hesitation. I thank Linda for her time before we leave, and after tonight, I'm making a mental note to research New York City real estate tomorrow morning.

# 26

## BECCA

I wake up to two strong arms holding me from behind. I breathe out a contented sigh.

*Julian.*

After a strong-willed debate, we agreed my place was the better option. The only one I have to worry about seeing us is Mrs. Goldstein… and maybe Daddy.

Julian kisses my shoulder and whispers, "Hey, baby."

"It's still a little weird, you calling me that," I say honestly. "We've only known each other for a week, two tops."

"Happy week and a half anniversary?"

I turn in his arms. "Julian, I'm serious."

"So am I."

He settles in closer to me, pulling my leg up and over his waist. I'm now hyperaware of the fact that his morning wood is inches from my *lady garden*. It should forever be called a lady garden, until we're old and gray. *What the fuck am I saying? Old and gray? Fuck. I'm in way too deep here.*

"Can we both just agree that all of this is completely unreasonable and run off into the sunset like one of your novels, *Merlot?* It would save us the time examining the absurdity of it all." He kisses my forehead and slowly runs his fingers up and down my arm. "I've been meaning to ask you, how did you come up with your pen name?"

"I love red wine and *Pride and Prejudice*," I answer simply.

He chuckles. "Seriously? That's it?"

"Yup," I reply, popping the 'p.'

"I fucking love yo— *it.* I love it."

"Oh no." I sit up, clutching the sheet to my chest. "You did not just say that."

The back of his head hits the pillow with force. "Yeah." He closes his eyes. "I did, didn't I?" Opening one of his eyes to check to make sure I'm still watching his reaction, he asks, "Would you be mad if I said I'm falling for you?"

"No." I reach over to my bedside table for my phone. I unlock it and type out a message. He eyes me curiously but I don't look up completely from my phone until the message notification lights up the screen. I toss it back onto the table. "Food poisoning."

"What?" He asks with a chuckle.

I bite my lip, trying to contain my amusement. "Food

poisoning. You can't record today because we both have food poisoning. Bad sushi."

"Oh, my Becca. What did you do?"

I shrug. "I have a hot man in my bed who is trying to profess his undying love for me. Why wouldn't I fake food poisoning so I could spend the day with him?"

"Undying love? As I recall, I only said I was falling for you."

"Admit it, my Julian. You're hopelessly and incandescently in love with me," I say with as much confidence as I can muster without laughing. My favorite Regency heroines would be proud.

"Even if I am, I'll never admit to it."

I frown. "Why the hell not?"

"Because you, my Becca, wouldn't believe me if I did. How could I tell this beautiful, naked woman wrapped up with me that I'm in love with her, and risk her not returning my feelings? No, that grand declaration will come at a later date."

"Now look who's suddenly the voice of reason," I chuckle and kiss him. "For the record, I look forward to this later date of yours."

---

Julian convinced me that we needed to record today. Since food poisoning is unpredictable, we were able to claim it passed and headed into the sound recording studio.

We have a larger room this time, but the close quarters are going to be difficult for me today. We're recording a scene where Bryan's brother, David, has Anna at his mercy. Hearing Julian recite the lines is going to do things for me. I have to control myself and not attempt to dry hump my narrator.

"*Chapter 9. David.*" He clicks his clicker twice to leave space for Anna's narration and to cue the engineer that his line is done. "*He calls you his kitten, but you're more of a lioness, Anna.*" Click click. "*I sit back in my chair, 'On your knees. Show me who you belong to.'*"

Almost immediately, I drop to my knees in front of him.

"Becca, what are you doing?"

"What does it look like I'm doing?" I look up at him with doe eyes, unzipping his pants

"I can't record when—" I free his cock and wrap my mouth around it. "*Fuck.*" He's too thick for me to take him deep, so I use my hands to make up for it. He strokes my cheek and pulls my hair back for me. "Be my good girl and let me fuck that pretty mouth of yours, baby." His grip on my hair tightens and I'm now incredibly wet. Something about how he said…

I pull off of him. "Say it again."

He groans and his hand strokes his incredibly hard cock. "Say what? I'll say whatever the hell you want me to, if it means I get that mouth on me again."

"*Good girl.* You need to say it just like that in the scene." I move from my knees and sit in the chair next to him, expectantly.

"You think I can record anything when my dick is hanging out and I just had the best almost-blowjob of my life?" When I don't reply, he takes a deep breath. "Fuck, fine. *Good girl.*"

I shake my head. "That's not it. Maybe draw it out?"

He adds inflection at the end. "*Good girl…*"

"No. That's not right. Emphasize the 'i'?"

"*Good gIrl.*" He tries not to laugh but it escapes him anyway.

I groan. "Just… do it the way you did it when you weren't in character."

"You were sucking me off, Becca. It's hard to replicate that." I glance down at his cock that he's still stroking and drop back down to my knees. "That's not what I meant. You don't have to—"

"Hmm," I hum against his hard length as I take him in my mouth. I pull off long enough to tell him, "Hit record."

"Fuck." He taps the button and attempts to resume the narration. "*That's my good girl, Becca…* Shit." I chuckle at his slip up. "*That's my good girl, Anna, taking me so well.*"

"I want you to come in my mouth, Julian." I continue licking and sucking, bringing him closer to the edge. His balls tighten and I know he's almost there.

"Baby, you feel so good." His praise eggs me on. "You're fucking perfect, taking my cock like this. Are you wet?" I nod with his cock still in my mouth. "Fuck." He tugs on my hair to pull me off of him. "Go in my bag and grab a condom."

Without a word, I reach into his laptop case and take one out, tear the foil with my mouth, and roll it onto his cock. I strip out of my leggings and panties and climb on top of him, lowering myself inch by thick inch. He thrusts up inside me, forcing me to take most of him. I take a deep breath and lower myself further.

"I just need a second."

"I know. You're doing so well, baby. Look at you taking all of me. You feel incredible. Just rock back and forth on me to help you adjust." I grind onto him. "Just like that," he hisses. "Fuck, I'm going to come if you keep that up."

"Isn't that the point?"

Julian kisses me and it's brutal and demanding. As he pulls back, he takes my bottom lip between his teeth before letting it go. "That's my good girl, keep grinding on me. I want you to use me to come." I do as he says and rock back and forth, taking him deeper. He pushes up into me, meeting my rhythm. I'm so deliciously full but he grips my hips and drives up harder. It's almost too much.

"I'm close," I gasp.

"I know, baby. Don't wait for me. Fuck me hard and come all over my cock." He reaches between us and pinches my clit, forcing me to come unexpectedly. "That's right. Show me who this pussy belongs to, baby. Say it. Tell me you're mine."

I haven't recovered from my orgasm and the words tumble from my lips, "I'm yours."

"That's right. You're mine, my Becca." He thrusts up into me a few times before letting out what can only be described as a roar with his own release. "*Fuck.*"

I chuckle but it's cut short. "*Shit!* Is that still recording?"

Julian glances over at the computer. "Yeah." He presses a few buttons. "It's deleted now. I don't want anyone but me to hear you coming."

"Too bad. That would've made for some great masturbation inspiration for me," I say with faux disappointment, even though I'm mostly worried about someone hearing me tell him I'm his.

"No need to touch yourself, baby. That's my job now. I'll gladly whisper dirty things to you with my hand between your legs."

I lift off him, genuinely impressed we didn't break the condom. He removes it, ties it off and tosses it into the trash. I look for my discarded underwear and leggings and put them on once I find them.

"What, are you going to stay over every night to ensure I'm sexually satisfied?" I joke as I get dressed.

Without an ounce of sarcasm, he replies, "Every. Single. Night."

# 27

# JULIAN

Last week, I spent my days in the studio and my nights in Becca's bed. I'm in a rush to complete this book so I can get out of the contract as soon as possible, so I'm working long hours every day. I'm exhausted but it's worth it.

Each morning, I wake up at 5am to get in a three mile run before I head straight to the studio for eight to ten hours a day. When I'm done, I rush home to her with dinner in hand if she's in the middle of writing or editing a chapter and doesn't have time to cook. I would never expect her to make dinner for us, but when I walk in to the smell of garlic or onions, my heart aches a little that this could be our norm. Only, it wouldn't be her cooking, it would be my personal chef preparing a meal for the two of us after a long day at work.

I'm almost done with the book. As soon as I finish, it'll be off to the engineer to put it together with the other narrator's work. The edits will take the longest, but I should be completely finished in less than a month.

One month and I can be with her, take her out, and show the world that she's mine.

After a particularly long day, I'm headed home to my girl. *My girl.* It doesn't feel like weeks with her, it feels like years. She buzzes me up to the apartment and I let myself in.

"Honey, I'm home," I jokingly call, as I've done for the last week. But I'm not joking. I'm never joking. I come up from behind and wrap my arms around her, kissing her shoulder. "Smells good."

"Nothing special, just chicken enchiladas and a salad." She shrugs. "Can you grab plates?"

"Sure." I kiss her neck and step away to take out a few plates from the cabinet and a couple beers from the fridge. We prep our plates and take a seat at her round kitchen table.

We sit in comfortable silence for several minutes before she breaks it. "How is the reconciliation chapter coming?" Becca asks between bites.

"Anna is a real bitch," I reply with a smirk. "How you managed to give her a happily ever after *and* readers were obsessed with it… you're fucking talented." She blushes. Bringing my beer to my lips, I add, "The book is almost done."

Eyes wide, she sets down her fork and wipes her mouth. "How? I thought you had at least five chapters left and the epilogue."

"Duet narration. The last few chapters are mostly Anna. I finished three today. So, I have a few more days of recording, then I'll go back through and fix anything I'm not in love with." I stand and make my way into the kitchen to get seconds of enchiladas and another beer. When I return, I kiss her softly before sitting back down. "One month, tops, and I'm done."

Becca chews on her lip. I know the question is coming; we haven't talked about it. I need to get back to California to wrap up a few things, but I'll come right back here as soon as it's all done. I haven't even been in New York for three weeks and I'm looking at apartments so I can be with her. I can work from anywhere and this is where I want to be.

"I forgot to tell you, I have to go upstate this weekend. I had plans to visit my family and, well, I got a little distracted by... all of this."

"Oh." I try not to sound disappointed that she's not inviting me.

"Would you—"

"Yes." Shit. I'm not disappointed. Worse, I'm fucking desperate.

"You didn't even know what I was going to ask." She bites her lip, a small smile tugging at the corner.

*Get it together.*

I drag my hand over my five o'clock shadow. "You're right. What were you going to ask?"

"Would you drive me to the train station?"

My face falls. "Oh, sure... I mean, yes, of course."

Becca lets out a full belly laugh. "I'm kidding." She stands and climbs onto my lap, straddling me. "Come with me."

"Is that a question or demand?" I keep my tone light. I shouldn't be this excited to go with her this weekend, but I fucking am. I'm beyond infatuated with this woman.

"Both. Will you? I know your answer is yes, but I just want to see you all wound up again."

I pinch her side and she yelps. "Yeah, I'll come with you. Speaking of which…" I pull her shirt over her head and toss it to the ground. She's wearing the lacy green bra that matches her eyes. I swear she wears it because she knows it's my favorite.

"Are you making an orgasm joke? I know you can do better than that."

I pull down the cups of her bra and tease her nipples with slow licks, grazing them with my teeth. I slip my hand into her sweatpants, pressing two fingers inside her. "Fuck, you're already wet for me." I remove them and suck them clean, groaning. "I didn't get to taste you yesterday, you were up late writing."

"I know. I'm sorry," she says sadly. I pause for a moment and pull her bra back up and over her perfect tits. "Whoa, wait… you can keep doing that!"

"I have no issue with you working late. You should never apologize for it." I bring her lips to mine.

"Okay," she whispers between kisses. "So, can you carry on with all your sexy talk and wanting to go down on me?"

*Fuck. I love her.*

I stand, wrap her legs tighter around me and walk to the bedroom. "I'll tell you all the things I didn't get to do to you last night while I play with this delicious pussy of yours."

"What about dinner?"

"You want more enchiladas? I'll fly us to Mexico in the morning. Right now, I need to hear you screaming my name as I make you come over and over again."

I set her on the bed and pull off my shirt. My fingers curl into her waistband as I trail kisses down her stomach. Her hands tangle in my hair and I only manage to pull her pants down an inch, when there's a knock at the door.

We both pause. "I didn't hear anything. You didn't hear anything, right?" she asks hopefully.

Three more knocks. I press a final kiss to her belly and grab my shirt. "I got it. It's probably just your neighbor telling us to keep it down, again."

She sighs and I make my way to the front door, putting on my shirt along the way. I check the peephole and, sure enough, it's Mrs. Goldstein.

I open the door to find her hand poised to knock again. "Oh, hello there, handsome. Is Becca around?"

"Sure, one second." Looking back into the apartment, I yell to Becca, "Hey, baby, it's Mrs. Goldstein."

There's rustling coming from the bedroom, the sound of drawers opening and closing. Becca walks out in an oversized sweatshirt and picks up her discarded shirt from earlier off the ground, tossing it at me. I can't help but chuckle.

"Hi. Everything okay?" she asks.

"I have to head out of town for the weekend. Could you take care of Daddy for me?"

"Oh." Becca winces. "I'm actually headed out of town for the weekend, too."

"Well, fucksticks. Do you know of anyone who can make sure Daddy doesn't get into trouble?" Mrs. Goldstein adjusts her glasses and looks at me expectantly.

"I'm going with Becca, otherwise I would be happy to help," I insist.

"I'm sorry, you two are obviously busy. I tried calling but you didn't pick up. I shouldn't have stopped by." She turns to head to her apartment.

Becca pokes her head into the hall. "Stop by anytime. Sorry I can't help! Next time, I'd love to spend time with Daddy."

Mrs. Goldstein turns. "Thank you, dear. Go have fun jumping that man's bones tonight. Oh, to be young again."

Becca and I laugh and close the door, but her laughter is cut short. "Shit. Where's my phone?" She walks into the kitchen where it's plugged into the wall. Yanking on the cord to remove it, she begins scrolling casually. A second later, though, her face goes white. "Crap, there's a lot of missed calls and…" Her hand flies to her mouth as she mutters, "No. *No, no, no*. This isn't happening."

I come up behind her. "What's wrong?"

"Check your phone." She shakes her head and waves me off as she reads. "You're CC'd… *Fuck!*"

I grab my laptop bag from the couch and pull out my phone, my eyes catching on an email that has Becca's book in the subject line.

---

**To**: Merlot Bennet

**CC**: Andre Stark, Julian Evans

**From**: Cassandra Wilson

**Subject**: FWD: MMC Narration - Delivery of Fate

Becca,

This email is to inform you that, per Andre's email below, Bryan North will be taking over the narration of *Delivery of Fate*. I am CC'ing Andre here to coordinate a meeting this week, or early next week with Bryan.

Julian - Thank you for all of your time on this project. It has been a pleasure working with you.

Regards,

Cassie Wilson

Sent from my phone

---

**To**: Cassandra Wilson

**CC**: Julian Evans

**From**: Andre Stark

**Subject**: MMC Narration - Delivery of Fate

Hi Cassandra,

There will be a narrator change for this project. Please let me know when you and Merlot are available for a meeting to transition the project from Julian Evans to Bryan North. We need this to be a smooth transition to get everything done in time.

Thank you,

Andre Stark

---

There are also texts from him.

ANDRE

Pick up your phone! You're off the Bennet book. Check your email.

It's for the best.

*Andre, what did you do?*

# 28

## BECCA

This isn't happening. No. There has to be some sort of mistake. I read and reread the emails over and over.

There's no mistake.

I'm in hell.

How did this happen?

*Hamilton… Fuck.*

"What the fuck is this?" Julian's voice sounds distant, even though he's only a few feet from me.

"I need to call Cassie," I mutter to myself. I finally look up from my phone. "What did you say to Andre when we saw him?"

"Nothing. He asked if I was sleeping with you, but I denied it." Julian rakes his hand through his hair, landing at the back of his neck and gripping it. "Fuck. This is my fault. I asked him about the fraternization policy a couple weeks back. It probably put a target on my back."

"I can't work with Bryan. If you aren't finishing the book, I need to see if John can still do it." I step toward him. "What did you ask about the policy?" I ask cautiously.

He drops his hand, shoving both in his pockets. "I was careless. I asked for it to be removed."

"When?"

"After St. Tropez," he replies, his voice barely above a whisper. "I'm sorry."

I wrap my arms around his middle. It takes him by surprise but he embraces me back, kissing the top of my head.

"I'm so sorry," he repeats, whispering into my hair. "I promise I won't let this hurt you. I'll take the blame for whatever fallout there is. I'll go back to California if I have to."

I pull back to look at him. "We don't even know what's going on yet. If there's any bad press from it, we'll go down together, okay?"

He kisses my forehead and pulls me back into his embrace. Being in his arms feels... *like home*. I need to get to the bottom of what happened; I can't risk losing him. I don't want him to go back to California. I want him here with me. I...

I'm in love with him.

"No," he growls. "I told you I wouldn't let this impact your career. If there's anything that could bring your book bad PR, I'll make sure it's all on me."

"I can't let you—"

"Yes, you can. Let me call Andre and send off a few dozen emails to see what's happening." He kisses my temple once before releasing me. "I'm going to head to the hotel and try to figure this out."

"Are you"—I swallow hard as tears prick behind my eyes —"coming back?"

Julian cups my cheeks, resting his forehead against mine. He brings my lips to his and a single tear escapes the corner of my eye.

"I love you, my Becca."

My eyes are glassy; I can hardly see straight. "Fuck. You can't say that. Not right now. Not when we're dealing with this."

"Too bad, I just did." He smirks and tucks my hair behind my ear. "I love you. I've loved you since the moment I took your hand on that plane. I knew you were special, I just didn't know how much. We're going to fix this so I can come back to you."

He kisses me again, but it isn't the same. It feels like good-bye, laced with sadness, not promises. When we break apart, I choke on a sob. He grabs his laptop bag and puts on his shoes. He walks out without another word.

*I'm a fucking idiot.*

The minute the door clicks shut, I fling it back open. "Julian." He turns, tears welling in his eyes. "I love you, too."

We both pause, as if… *time stops, they feel a zing course through their bodies, the air crackles between them, their breath hitches.*

"I love you, Julian." It comes out as a strangled whisper.

"I know."

Julian closes the distance and glides his hand into my hair. His mouth finds mine in a delicate kiss, and I chuckle against his lips. "Really? *That's* the response I get? A *Star Wars* reference?"

"There's nothing else to say. This wasn't a 'guy falls first' trope. It was love at first sight, fated mates, instalove… Am I missing any?" I shake my head, unable to hide my smile. "Didn't think so. We fell together, my Becca. I know you love me as much as I love you."

He steps back and heads down the stairs. Once he's out of view, I blink away the love-drunk haze.

*Cassie.* I need to fix this.

It's been four hours. Four excruciating hours and he won't return my calls or texts.

Cassie claimed that because Bryan and Julian are under the same agency, Andre included a clause that they reserved the right to swap out narrators without notice. I didn't believe her, so I pulled up the contract. Sure enough, there it was in black and white. It was written with the intention that, if something happened to a narrator, the agency wouldn't lose the contract, but this is some shady shit.

My phone rings in my hand. I don't check the caller ID before picking up. "Julian? Are you coming home?"

"No, kitten, but if you need to roleplay, that can be arranged."

My stomach drops and all the blood drains from my face. "Bryan," I grit out. It's the middle of the night. Why is he calling me?

Bryan laughs. It makes me want to strangle him through the phone. "Sorry about the whole switcheroo, baby. That little narrator friend of yours should've been more careful, openly claiming you in front of me." He tsks. "Amateur."

"What the fuck are you talking about?"

"You should've just let me fuck you at that restaurant and you'd still have your little fantasy voice actor. If I couldn't have *Delivery of Fate*, your pussy would've been a satisfactory consolation prize."

I comb through the memories of that day: the panel interview, the restaurant, Julian and I at the VIP event… *Fuck.*

"I'll take your silence as acceptance that I'll be doing the narration work. Just wanted to check in to see if you wanted me to pop by, you know, for old time's sake?"

"You're disgusting." I hang up.

Bile rises in my throat and I rush over to my sink, throwing up the contents of my stomach until I'm only dry heaving.

My phone vibrates on the counter next to the sink; Julian's name pops up on the screen.

I wipe my mouth and answer it. "It was Bryan," I say at the same time he says, "Becca, it was Andre."

"What?" I ask. "What was Andre?"

"I fired him. He's the one that made the switch. Someone tipped him off that I was seeing you after the book convention. *Hamilton* confirmed it, and he gave the project to Bryan. I was able to get John to take on the book, so you don't have to work with the asshole. Bryan will probably get an email in the morning. I'm sorry, baby. It's the best I could do."

*"Now boarding first class passengers for flight 374 to Los Angeles."*

No.

"Julian, where are you?"

"I love you, my Becca." He hangs up.

"This isn't how our story ends," I sob into my quiet apartment. I try calling him back but it goes straight to voicemail.

I call Amanda and she picks up on the third ring.

"Bitch, it's the middle of the night. You're lucky I'm finishing up edits on my book and not getting railed by some hot man."

"He's gone," I blurt out.

"Who's gone?"

"Julian. He… we got caught and they swapped out the narrator for *Bryan*."

"What?" she shrieks. "Fuck. I'm on my way."

# 29

## JULIAN

My group is called. *"Now boarding first class passengers for flight 374 to Los Angeles."*

"Julian, where are you?"

My heart breaks. I can't tell her. I can't get the truth out. "I love you, my Becca." I hang up and pull up my airline app to scan my ticket.

I approach the ticket scanner. "Have a great flight, sir," he says and I head down the ramp.

*No, it's not going to be a great flight. I'm leaving the woman I love in New York.*

My phone vibrates with an incoming call. *My Becca.* I turn it off and pocket it. I can't let her know the sacrifice I made—she would hate me for it. If she doesn't hate me, she might do something that could damage her career. I can't let that happen.

I take my seat and stow my laptop. A couple approaches and the woman takes the seat next to me. I recognize her but can't place her. Maybe she just has a familiar face?

"Excuse me. I'm so sorry to ask, but my friend and I were wondering if you wouldn't mind switching places with me so I could have the aisle?" the woman asks.

"Oh, sure. If you want, I can trade your friend so you can sit together?" I offer.

"Really? That would be amazing. We couldn't get seats next to each other so would have to pass notes like high school during the flight," she chuckles.

The man is about to take his seat when the woman stops him, "Ethan, we can sit together. Do you want aisle or window?" I feel like I've met him before, but I can't place it.

"I'll take… oh, hi there. Julian, right?" he asks with a wide smile. I stand and trade him seats. "You're doing the narration for Merlot Bennet?"

"Yeah, I was. I'm sorry, have we met?"

He offers his hand as he sits. "Ethan Barlowe. We were at the convention a few weeks ago and met briefly at the VIP event."

"Right. I thought you looked familiar."

"I'm Emma." She reaches across Ethan to shake my hand and sits back into her seat. "I'm sorry, did you say you *were* the voice actor? Are you done with the book? That's exciting," she says with a beaming smile.

My face falls. "No, I can't say much, only that I'm no longer a narrator for the book."

"Oh shit." Ethan's eyes are wide. "Sorry, that sucks. Can you say who's doing it now?"

I shake my head. John has the contract in place but it's not public yet. There was no way in hell I'd let Bryan within a thousand feet of her.

Emma's scrolling her phone and gasps. "It's everywhere. Shit." She whispers something to Ethan and they trade spots so she can talk to me. "Look, this is unorthodox," she tells me, "I know you probably have representation, but if you need anything, let me know. I run a literary agency and might be able to help."

*Fuck. What now?*

I take out my phone and power it on. Emma sits back in her seat and talks to Ethan as a few passengers pass down the aisle between us to find their seats. The moment my phone is on, it's inundated with hundreds of notifications—texts, emails, voicemails, and media outlets.

It was only off for a few minutes. How is this possible?

### *Billionaire Voice Actor Beds Erotica Novelist*

### *Begging for the Billionaire Author Finds Billionaire of Her Own*

### *Handsy at Hamilton: Best-Selling Romance Author Cozies Up to Narrator for Upcoming Release*

The headlines only get worse from there. All of them blaming Becca.

I pull up one of them and read that Bryan is announced as her new narrator. That's not the worst of the story. It's Becca. She's painted as someone who was with me for my money. The irony being that she has no idea how well off I actually am. I've worked very hard to keep it quiet.

*Well, she knows now.*

There's a string of messages from her.

> **MY BECCA**
>
> Don't leave NY
>
> Please
>
> I know your phone is off or you're sending me to voicemail. If you see this, please don't believe what the news is saying.
>
> Your net worth is $60 billion?!
>
> That explains a lot.

There are four more messages but I don't get to them because there's an incoming call from her. I blow out a deep breath and answer.

"Hey, baby."

"Don't you *hey, baby* me, mister. *Sixty billion,* Julian? And you let me make you chicken enchiladas. Oh shit, I made you pot roast one night. That's like… peasant food. I fed you peasant food. And you let me!"

I chuckle, even though none of this is funny. "I don't know what happened in the last five minutes since I talked to you. It's fucking everywhere." I glance over to Emma and Ethan, who are talking to each other and hopefully not eavesdropping. "I'm sorry. I thought I made this go away. I'll take care of it."

"Made what go away? You're not making any sense."

Bryan or Andre are behind this. No one else would go to the trouble.

"I'll call you in the morning once I have it sorted out. They'll pay dearly for this." My vein is throbbing in my forehead and a rumble comes from my chest. "No one fucks with my girl and gets away with it."

"You're getting all growly, which, don't get me wrong, is hot as hell. But, what is there to sort out? This is out there in the universe. Please, Julian, you have to give me something here."

The flight attendant signals to me to hang up. "I've gotta go. I love you, my Becca." I click 'end call' before I do something reckless like run back to her, ruining everything I put in place. I know she loves me, but hearing it is entirely different.

I look back over at Ethan and Emma, still whispering to each other. I can't make out all of it but I do manage to hear "pen name" and "fucking adorable."

*Shit.*

"So, I know you saw the headlines," I tell them. Emma looks up and nods, chewing her lip. "I—"

"We're about to pull back from the gate, can I get any of you a drink?" the flight attendant interrupts.

Emma orders a gin and tonic with extra lime. Ethan has an old fashioned. And I order my usual Manhattan, wishing I was ordering one for Becca.

"You were saying?" Emma probes once the flight attendant walks away.

"Right. I'm currently without representation. I know this is a publicity nightmare but if you're looking to take on a new client, I'd love to be considered. I figure anyone who is down to take shots with my girl at a book convention is someone I should be working with."

Ethan laughs. "So, you *do* remember us."

"It took me a minute, but yeah, I do."

"So, what are you going to do about this Bryan guy taking over the narration? What an asshole. His panel interview that day was absolute trash. I hope that squeaky grocery cart has the day he deserves," Ethan says flippantly.

Emma smacks Ethan's shoulder and tells me, "What he *meant* to say was that we have a flight connection in LA; my office is in San Francisco. If you're up for the trip, I can have paperwork drafted before we arrive."

"Should have tripped him at that VIP event when I had the chance, or at least signed him up for a bunch of spam websites," Ethan grumbles. Emma hits his shoulder again. "What? A little chaos never hurt anyone."

# 30

# BECCA

"I've gotta go. I love you, my Becca."

"Wait—"

Julian hangs up. *Asshole.*

Sixty *fucking* billion dollars. What the actual hell is going on? My phone keeps vibrating with incoming messages and calls. Overwhelmed, I put it on 'do not disturb' since the one person I need to talk to right now is on a plane.

After pacing my apartment for twenty minutes, Amanda calls up using the intercom downstairs.

"I've got wine, more wine, and a few slices of pizza from the place down the street. Let me up," she says with a laugh. I buzz her up and unlock my door. A minute later, she barrels into my apartment. "All right, so am I going to kill him off in my next book? I'll name him Julian. Don't tempt me." She makes herself at home, setting everything down on my counter.

"We're not killing anyone off in your book," I insist as she plates our pizza. "Did you see the gossip rags?"

"Of course I did." She shovels a giant bite of pizza into her mouth and continues while chewing, "Sixty billion?"

"Why am I so stuck on that? I feel lied to, even though he never lied."

"St. Tropez, bitch. *St. Tropez*. What man plans a trip to France for, what, twenty-four hours—all because it was in your book? A fucking billionaire. That's who." She pours two glasses of wine, spilling a little on the counter and wiping it up with a paper towel. "So, what do we know? Layla is still in town, should we have her over and play a live version of Clue? She just finished writing that thriller, I'm sure she's watched enough crime dramas to figure this shit out."

"Seriously? He didn't kill anyone. He just didn't tell me he was loaded and then bailed on me. Fuck. I'm so stupid. I fell for him; I knew I would. Those damn golden flecks in his eyes and that stubble that comes in way too fast... fucking asshole." Amanda hands me a glass of wine and my pizza, then sits next to me on the couch. "The stupid part is that he told me he loves me *after* shit hit the fan."

"Do you love him?"

I blow out a long breath and gulp down my wine. "Yeah. I do. I know it's ridiculous; we've only known each other for a few weeks. We just... we had something special, you know?"

"So, go to him. Do one of those romcom airport scenes. *No, stop the plane!*"

"Oh, no, I've got it." I clear my throat. "*There are no flights. She's determined. Approaching the car rental counter, she begs and pleads to the attendant for the last available car.* It's a giant SUV and she's five foot and a hundred pounds wet. So, it's funny. *The man hands her the keys and she runs to her chariot to chase after the man she loves.*"

Amanda doubles over in laughter. "Okay, so you *have* to write that book. Hell, you need to write your story with Julian. Boy meets girl on a plane. He ends up doing her audiobook. They have incredible sex and fall in love... You have to write it. Maybe change his name though." She gives me a side eye for keeping Bryan's name in the book.

"I, uh... already kind of started it," I admit.

She sets down her wine and gestures for my laptop. "Let's see it! Since when am I not alpha reading all your work? Who do you have on the side?"

"No one," I answer honestly. "I just don't know if I'll publish it."

I power on my laptop and hand it to her. It's only a few chapters so I head into the kitchen to refill our wine and let her skim my work in progress.

"Becs, this... this is good. You have to publish it. But, I'm serious, change the name. What about Walter?"

"You're not serious..."

"Of course not." She raises her voice an octave and adds, "Oh, Wally, your cock is so huge!"

I can't help but laugh, but my laughter is cut short when I have a flashback to the plane and the banter with Julian about Stewart. *Is everything going to be ruined for me, now that he's gone?*

"What's wrong?"

"Nothing," I lie.

"Go to him."

"It's not that simple." *I wish it were.*

Amanda stands up and grabs her phone out of her purse. "You love him. He loves you, unless… Did he say otherwise?"

"No."

"All right." She returns her attention to her phone, typing and swiping for far too long.

"What are you doing?"

"We're going to LA. Tomorrow. 7am. Better get your beauty rest, we need to be up in four hours. Rideshares to get us there on time are going to be at a premium, and we aren't rolling in sixty billion dollars. Oh! Hold on." She swipes the phone twice and presses something before holding it to her ear. "You up for an adventure Layla-love? We're headed to LA to go run after a hot audiobook narrator. Yep, that's the one. See you at the airport, babe."

"He left. He probably doesn't want to see me."

"Liar. What was the last thing he said to you?"

"I love you... *my Becca*." My heart sinks as I repeat his words.

"Pack your bags, or I'll only pack lacy thongs for you and you can show up topless for him wearing only a scrap of fabric covering your pussy. We're going to LA."

# 31

# JULIAN

"Shit, that's my husband. One second." Emma takes her call away from Ethan and I as we wait for our bags.

"Tell Mayo I said hi!" Ethan yells to her as he walks away. *Mayo?* He looks back and laughs at the confusion on my face. "Long story. Anyway, if you're up for it after signing the contracts, my wife is supposed to meet me downtown for a quick lunch. You're welcome to join us."

"Sure, I have a few hours to kill before I fly back to LA." Following them to San Francisco wasn't in the plans, but if it gets me one step closer to putting all of this behind me and getting back to Becca, I'd go so far as to fucking move here.

My bag makes its way in front of me on the carousel as Emma returns. "Sorry about that. My daughter just graduated from college and her flight was moved up. She's supposed to be landing in the next half hour. Do you mind if we wait for her? I promised I'd pick her up."

I shrug. "I don't mind. Today, I'm sort of just along for the ride." I'd do just about anything for them. They're saving my ass since I'm sure I'm blacklisted at this point.

"I knew I liked this guy." Ethan pats me on the back. "I bet everyone is going to be hungry. Why don't I call Keith and see if he can open early for us? Julian can review the contract, and Emma and Harriet won't get hangry."

Emma mulls it over. "That works. I'll have my assistant meet us there."

"Is Robbie in town? Should we invite him?" he asks Emma.

She shakes her head. "No, they're playing Cincinnati tonight, he's supposed to fly in tomorrow morning... Sorry, Julian. My daughter is dating"—she looks around and lowers her voice—"Robbie Chavez. He's traveling this week and wants to surprise Harriet tomorrow."

"Robbie Chavez?" I ask. "The third baseman?" She nods. "No shit? He's having a hell of a year."

"If you say so," Ethan says, not looking up from his phone. He glances up briefly. "Sorry, I don't follow base-ball. Okay, so we're good to go. Mel's taking the girls to the aquarium, so I'll grab a quick bite with you before meeting up with them."

Emma checks her phone. "We have enough time for a quick coffee before she lands. Come on, my treat, Mr. Billionaire Narrator."

*Fuck. This is going to be my life now, isn't it?*

We grab a coffee and wait for Emma's daughter. For the next half hour, I listen to Emma and Ethan laugh and joke. It's obvious these two have known each other for most of their lives. The banter between the two of them has kept a smile on my face that has been gone since I had Becca on her bed ready to—

"Oh shit, she just got done with customs. You guys good to go, or do you need a refill for the road?" Emma asks, shaking her cup.

"I'm good, thank you." Ethan takes her cup to throw them away and I finish mine before tossing mine in the trash as we walk out. There's a newspaper sitting right on top with a headline:

### *Merlot Bennet Upgrades to a Billionaire Voice Actor.*

I have to fix this.

---

Emma's daughter, Harriet, is an aspiring YA fantasy novelist. The whole ride to the restaurant, she was beaming with excitement to discuss various books I've narrated. She's listened to almost all of them, which just gives me more assurance that working with Emma is going to be the best professional choice moving forward.

"If I publish, will you narrate one of my books?" Harriet asks hopefully.

"I think what you meant to say is *when* you publish. Manifest it, Harry," Ethan interrupts with a wink.

"Ugh. I hate when you call me that," she grumbles.

"Your dad isn't here for me to mess with, I need to have fun somehow," Ethan says with a shrug.

"You're a grown ass man, Ethan. As funny as your colorful insults are for my husband, don't make me tell Mel on you for teasing a woman half your age." Emma narrows her eyes.

"*Fine.*" Ethan rolls his eyes. "So, Harriet, as I was saying, don't sell yourself short. I know you don't want to use your connections to get published, but you need to be in the right mindset to let it happen."

"You're right," Harriet replies and turns to me. "So, I suppose I should rephrase. *When* I publish, I would love it if you would narrate one of my books."

I chuckle. "I'm sure that could be arranged, seeing as one of Emma's agents might be representing me."

Emma's phone vibrates on the table and she picks it up. I watch her suck in a breath. "Don't check your phone," she says to me with wide eyes.

My shoulders slump. Could today get any worse? "Lay it on me."

"Your emails were leaked. All that legwork you put in to protect Merlot... I need to get legal on this. You should call your lawyer as well. As soon as you're under contract, I can help with the professional side, but you'll want to protect yourself." Emma scrolls her phone while I pull out mine to contact my attorney.

"Excuse me, I just need a few minutes." I leave the table and head outside. My ears are ringing; my heart feels like it's going to jump out of my chest. This was all for nothing. Maybe I can fly to upstate New York? Becca should be headed there tomorrow. We can avoid the press and…

No. We need to face this head on.

I call Larry, ignoring the missed calls and texts from Becca. As much as I desperately need to hear her voice right now, I have to fix this first. After several minutes of him berating me for trying to fix this myself, he assures me that the only thing he can do is move forward with lawsuits against my former agent and Bryan. It's not enough.

I don't understand why they want to tarnish Becca's reputation, if Bryan was supposed to take over the narration. Bad press is *not* good for any brand, especially for an author. I pocket my phone and head back inside to give Emma the less than stellar news.

As I approach I catch the last part of the conversation. Emma tells Ethan, "Either bring them all here or swap out with her."

"Everything okay?" I ask, though I have a feeling it's anything but.

Emma blows out a long breath. "Yes, it will be. My sister-in-law is a corporate lawyer and can help me with moving some things along. Our legal team is down a person for maternity leave, so I'm hoping Mel can either meet us or Ethan can take the girls to the aquarium."

I rub my eye and blink a few times, reeling and hardly able to keep up after the flight and constant barrage of bad news. "I'm sorry, I don't know that I'm following. You're sister-in-law is—"

"His wife," she confirms.

"Got it. Well, I just got off the phone with Larry. I can sue for damages but that's about the extent of it," I say, defeated.

"I need to know what happened. You mentioned a few times that you put things in motion, and I understand wanting contracts in place first, but I want to get ahead of this. Are you comfortable sharing?" Emma asks.

Before I can reply, Ethan interjects. "Mel is ten minutes out. Being a lawyer, she would tell you to not say anything. But, seeing as all of your dirty laundry is already out there in the universe, it's ultimately up to you."

"I—" My phone lights up with My Becca. "Excuse me. I need to take this."

I answer as I begin walking out front again. "Hey, baby."

"Where are you?" Her voice sounds frantic.

"I'm in San Francisco meeting with a new agency. Why?"

"Because I'm standing outside of your house."

"My… You're in Temecula?" *Why is she in Temecula?*

"There's press here. I… I don't know what to do. Amanda tried to get another rideshare, but—"

"Stay there. I'll call my driver to pick you up," I insist. "It's going to be okay. Is it just the two of you? Any luggage."

"Layla is here, too. We each have a small bag. Mine is extra light because *someone* packed it for me," she grits out.

"*You'll thank me later, Julian,*" someone in the background says. It must be Amanda.

I rake a hand through my hair. "I can't believe you're there. All right, one minute and I'll have it all arranged."

"Okay. I lo—"

"I know, baby. I'll text you the details. I love you, my Becca."

I hang up.

# 32

# BECCA

"This asshole refuses to let me tell him that I love him." I pocket my phone and moments later the gate swings open for his property.

Layla chuckles. "Well, better than you being the one always saying it."

"I know you love me." His voice scares the crap out of me as it comes through the intercom next to the gate. We all jump. "Now, get inside. They won't follow you, it's private property." It clicks off as quickly as it came on.

"Do as the man says, Becs. We need to get away from these guys," Amanda says, ushering me through the tall bronze gates and away from the lurkers. "Damn, this guy is extra."

Layla chuckles. "Can we just stay here and have a writer's retreat?"

"I mean…" I shrug with a smirk.

I'm in awe as we approach the house. It's like something out of a movie. No. Out of a book. A movie wouldn't do this house justice. It reminds me of some of the homes that lined the beach in St. Tropez. It has the same neutral color pallet and sienna roof. There are a few white pillars in the entryway and a small fountain in front. As we walk up the way up the entirely too long pathway to the house, my breathing and heart rate increase.

I'm nervous.

I'm never nervous.

*What if I break something? Is it a museum in there?*

We make our way to the front door of this ridiculously large house. It's not a house. It's a damn mansion. Of course it is. *Sixty fucking billion dollars.* I shake my head. He stayed at my place for the past week when he could have been someplace like this?

"Hello?" My voice echoes against the marble floors and the ceilings that rival a small building in height.

Amanda and Layla move further into the house, passing a large staircase and into the kitchen. It's entirely too quiet and… *clean.* Way too clean for a bachelor. I internally roll my eyes; this is excessive.

"No one's here, Becs. What do you say you text Julian and let him know we're all moving in? I'm sure he wouldn't even notice we were here. My guess is fifty-three bedrooms and double the amount of baths," Amanda says, plopping down on the large leather sofa in the adjacent living room.

Layla checks the fridge. "It's definitely a bachelor pad. Condiments and more condiments." She closes it and peers into the pantry while I walk toward the back sliding glass doors.

"He's been in New York for a month. What did you expect? A farmer's market in the fridge?" I deadpan.

When I step outside, there's an olympic-size swimming pool, a small house to the right of it that could fit two of my apartments inside of it, and a large covered patio with a barbecue built into the island. About to set down my phone and purse, I spot a message from Julian.

> JULIAN
>
> Stay there. I'll be home later tonight.
>
> Please.

I reply back, biting my lip.

> And if I don't?

My phone vibrates in my hand moments after I hit send.

"Yes, Mr. Billionaire?" I answer.

"I'm serious. I need to know you're safe if there's media or anything outside. Please just stay there." His voice is quiet, nearly a whisper, but pleading.

"Okay, I'll stay, but"—I lower my voice—"why are we whispering?"

"One second." There's a muffle over the receiver but I can still make out, "Sorry, it's Bec... *Merlot*. Is it okay if I... Thanks." There's a pause followed by his voice at normal volume. "Okay. Is that better?" His voice is sultry, though I'm sure it's unintentional. Unfortunately, it's doing things to my nether regions.

"Yeah," I breathe, then clear my throat. "I mean, yes. Thank you."

"I'll be there tonight." It doesn't seem to phase him that I'm hot and bothered when all of this shit is happening around us. "I flew to San Francisco to sign contracts with a new agency. I could've done it electronically, but I wanted a chance to get to know Emma a little bit before I committed. She's been great. Her friend, Ethan, on the other hand, would probably make a great character for your next novel."

I pause for a brief moment. *Emma? Ethan?* Fuck, I don't know why but those names are ringing alarm bells for me.

"Emma? She's a literary agent?"

"Yeah," he replies.

"Shit. I think I met them. That Ethan guy, does he look like a Bradley Cooper doppelganger?"

Julian chuckles. "Now that you mention it, he kind of does. You met them at the Book Love."

"I remember them. Hang on." I rummage through my purse and find a business card. "Emma Alexander?"

"Yeah, that's her."

Now I'm the one laughing. "I liked her. Him more, but she was great. They're going to represent you?"

"She is. Or rather, her agency. That's the plan, at least."

I take a deep breath. "Okay. So, what next? How do we get rid of the people outside of your house… but also Bryan and Andre?"

"I'll take care of it." I'm about to reply but he beats me to it. "It wasn't just empty words. I love you. I'd move heaven and earth to protect you and your career from those assholes. They're going to pay dearly for what they've done."

Wrapped up in his romantic declarations, looking out at the pool calling my name, I reply, "On one condition."

"Dare I ask?"

"You don't hang up before I tell you something."

He chuckles and my chest is warm, feeling his laugh around me as if he were here. "Sure," he replies.

"You know this is ludicrous, we've hardly known each other for a month."

"I'm hanging up now."

"I love you, Julian." I blurt out.

"I know, baby. Don't let this bullshit get to you. I love you so damn much. Since I've been away from you, it's like a piece of me is gone. When I've fixed everything, I just hope you'll still love me after what I've done. I'll always be yours, my Becca."

The line goes dead before I can question it. I stare at my phone in disbelief and try to call him back but am sent to his voicemail.

*After what he's done? What did he do?*

I look out at the pool, feeling like I have no control in this whole thing.

I want things to go back to the way they were when a hot man whisked me off to the other side of the world. He did something that he thinks I'll be pissed off about… I don't care about any of it. I should, but my emotional exhaustion is taking a toll. I don't want to feel right now.

I want St. Tropez. I want a man who looks at me like I'm his whole world. I want to swim in the clear blue waters and let it wash away every bad thing that's happened since I saw that email from Cassie.

I strip out of my pants and shirt, leaving only my bra and underwear. I run toward the pool, diving in without checking the temperature. I'm going to take back my joy.

The pool is practically bath water. Yet another thing I shouldn't be surprised about, but am. I swim in slow broad strokes. When I reach the end, I pull up onto the side, resting my arms on top of the concrete.

Reality hits me like a bullet train with no conductor. I attempt to center my breathing, wishing with all my being that the last twenty-four hours was all just one bad dream… minus the swimming in a billionaire's pool. He's trying to fix something that my agent says can't be fixed without a lawsuit.

There are giggles, followed by two splashes behind me, as Amanda and Layla cannonball into the pool. They swim over to me and, as fucked up as all of this is, I try to appreciate the fact that I'm here with two of my favorite people.

"You thought I was kidding about moving in here. Bitch, you're stuck with me. I'm never leaving," Amanda says as she slides up next to me, leaning on the edge of the pool.

"We can't up and move to California. Well, Layla can. At least she is on this coast."

"*Ahem,*" Layla clears her throat dramatically as she settles on the other side of Amanda. "We're authors, we can live anywhere," she challenges.

"Julian actually joked that he would move to New York after the book narration was done," I sigh, shaking my head. "How could I fall so fast for him? I had no clue he lived in a fucking mansion or that he—"

"You write romance," Amanda interrupts. "Let yourself believe in what you write for ten seconds. You can have a happily ever after. Just please don't get married and have babies in the epilogue. It's a little cliche."

"Why shouldn't I marry or have babies with Julian? *What am I saying?* This isn't a romance novel, this is my life! I've known this man for a month. Stop trying to make this more than it is. Shit went down because someone outed us. He says he's going to fix it and will be here tonight, so I'm sure we'll figure it out but I'm not even thinking about moving in with this man, much less marrying and having kids with him."

The girls exchange a look before Layla asks, "Tonight?"

"Yeah. He said he'd be here tonight. Why?"

Amanda chuckles. "Well, as much as we'd love to be here for that epic fuckfest, Layla and I will find other accommodations."

"There will *not* be an epic fuckfest," I insist, rolling my eyes.

"When you see the email leak, there will be," Amanda says with a smirk.

## JULIAN

The email leak is bad.

Not for Becca.

Not for her books.

For my relationship with Becca.

The world now knows the lengths I went to, to protect her. I just hope she'll forgive me for overstepping. I'm being painted as a real life romance hero, but I don't think she'll see it that way. Whoever leaked it wanted to hurt me. In the world of romance books, it had the opposite effect.

"I offered to buy out the contract for *Delivery of Fate*," I tell Emma.

"I saw," she says cautiously.

"But you don't know why."

Ethan chuckles. "Sorry, but the entire internet kind of saw why."

"Breach of contract is no joke, Ethan," Emma says sternly.

"I know. Becca knows. We had a relationship... *have* a relationship. I'm in love with her. I don't care what it costs me financially; I want all of this gone. John agreed to take on the book, which prompted Andre or Bryan to leak the emails. I wasn't thinking... I was trying to protect her, but I made it worse." If they hadn't seen the emails themselves, I wouldn't be divulging any of this, but it feels good to get it off my chest all the same.

Ethan pats my shoulder in solidarity. "The terms you agreed to in that contract are probably null and void since they leaked the emails. Mel can confirm it when she gets here." He shakes his head. "I mean, I'm all for a grand gesture, but I could never agree to what you did. Lucky for you, Mel's the best corporate lawyer on the west coast. I'm not just saying that because she's my wife. She might be able to salvage some of this." Ethan finishes his drink and signals for another. "Don't judge, I'm headed to a water zoo with two small children. Liquid courage is necessary."

"Where are your keys?" I boldly ask.

"Relax, Gatsby. You're not the only rich guy at the table here," he playfully scoffs. "I would never drink and drive. My driver, Doug, should be here any minute now with my girls."

I breathe a sigh of relief. "Fair enough."

"If you want, I can take them," Harriet offers. "I know Cat wants to hear about the edits I made to my book anyway."

An idea strikes me at the mention of her book. She writes YA fantasy... I'm a fantasy narrator... If I'm announced on another project, some of the press will pivot away from Becca and her book.

"How far along are you on your manuscript?" I blurt out.

All eyes on me, Harriet replies, "It's done... ish."

"Indie?"

"For now," she replies confidently.

"Edited?"

"Of course."

"Who do you have in mind for female narration?" I ask.

"Kimberly Croft," she says without hesitation.

"Funding?" I can afford to front it without question, but as an up-and-coming author, I want to be sure she's prepared to go toe-to-toe with other authors without having an in with her agent mom, or being funded by me.

Harriet looks to Emma, who replies with a smirk, "Her dad can line up investors in the next day or so." Eyes twinkling, Harriet exudes all of the joy that I miss from Becca. She's beaming with excitement.

"It might be a good move to announce that I have a new project. Don't you agree?" I don't try to hide my smile, but it falls when it hits me that Becca's book isn't done. "I want to finish Becca... *Merlot's* book but I don't think that's in the cards."

"Oh, for fuck's sake. We figured out her name was Becca hours ago. *My Becca*. Really? Think that wouldn't slip past a few avid romance readers?" Ethan deadpans.

"This asshole calls his woman 'princess,' as if you couldn't get any more cliché than that," Harriet adds, side eyeing Ethan. "So, he has no room to talk."

I laugh and it's lighter than I've felt since I last saw Becca. "Well, what term of endearment did you come up with for the character in your book? Assuming there's a love interest."

Harriet lifts her chin with pride. "Beautiful."

"That's sweet," I say, honestly.

"It's what my dad's always called Emma," Harriet says with a shrug. "I always thought it was romantic that he never called her by her real name when they reconnected after so many years apart." Emma blushes with a soft smile. I make a mental note to tell Becca all this, once the dust settles, so she can ask Emma about this second chance romance of hers.

I clear my throat. "Well, if we can get the contracts in place, I feel like it would be great for all parties involved. My lawyers are trying to do damage control for the email leak, but how can I help Becca?" Ethan looks down, chuckling. "What?" I ask him.

"Go get your woman," he says, clucking his tongue. "Life's too fucking short. Hell, my brother-in-law wasted sixteen years of his life... Not that you're a waste, Harriet. You're a fucking treasure... But he was a fucking idiot and it took that long for him to get his head out of his ass. Take her somewhere while Emma's company fixes this for you. Maybe a week in Milan? Scuba diving in Australia? Ooo, I know, what about taking her to—"

"St. Tropez." We speak at the same time.

"Just like her book," he adds.

We didn't get to sightsee when we were there—I spent the entire time inside her, but I don't regret a second of it. He's right; if I take her away for a while, the press will die down and our lawyers can handle everything.

*The contract. The fucking contract with Andre.*

My face falls. "I can't take her. I'm not even supposed to be seen with her. Right now, she's at my place in Temecula and, if I'm spotted with her, I'll be slapped with a lawsuit."

"Use a pseudonym. No one will be looking for you in St. Tropez." Ethan shrugs.

A pregnant woman tosses her purse onto the chair beside me and sits next to Ethan. "Okay, you summoned me." She looks around and when she lays eyes on me, she asks, "Julian?" I nod. "Well, you'll have to forgive my mom attire. I didn't know I'd be saving a billionaire from his failed grand gesture today."

Ethan places his arm on the back of her chair, kisses her temple, and rests his hand on her belly. "Hey, princess. Where are the girls?"

"In the car," she replies.

Ethan stands, offers me his hand. "Great seeing you again. Good luck," he says with a wink and heads for the door.

"All right, get me up to speed… and some nachos. Nachos first, then tell me who we're destroying today."

My hair is still dripping wet and my clothes are soaked. I don't fucking care. I'll clean up the mess on the floor later.

For the last hour, I've read and reread the leaked emails on my phone. Julian hasn't returned any of my calls, leaving me restless.

*I'll pay whatever you want. Name your price. I'll buy out the contract. I'll fund the whole thing.*

*If it means you won't go after Becca, I'll even agree to not be seen with her until after the audiobook releases.*

*If you hurt her reputation, in any way, you can kiss yours goodbye.*

As I stare at the screen, reeling from the words in the emails, an incoming call from Julian makes me jump.

I answer. "What the fuck, Julian?" There's silence on the other end. "Hello?"

"You saw them," he says calmly. It's not a question. I shake my head, my anxiety building.

"You agreed to not be seen in public with me until it's released? Why would you do that?"

"Because I'm in love with you!" Julian roars, then pauses, sighing. His voice calmer, he continues, "I'd sacrifice everything I have, if it meant that we wouldn't need to sneak around anymore when this is over."

My heart stops. Everything has been so fast with him. I'm not sure I ever even had the chance to properly process our epic first meeting, let alone every whirlwind moment after that... and now there's this. I take a moment to marinate with what he did. "I don't care about the audiobook," I say, mostly to myself.

"Yes, you do, bitch!" Amanda calls from the kitchen as she pulls a bottle of white wine from the fridge.

"I really don't. Not anymore. It's not like it's for one of my new releases, it's a re-released title for a book that I shouldn't have written in the first place." I shake my head. I'm getting off track. "That doesn't change the fact that you offered to pay for the whole project and went so far as to include verbiage in the contract that would"—my breath catches—"keep us apart for months." Julian is quiet, so I continue. "This, you and me, is so new. You would choose to walk away from this for the sake of a fucking audiobook?"

"Walk away? Fuck no. I got cocky. It was supposed to be temporary and it seemed like a small price to pay. I knew that Andre could put Bryan on it, so I reached out to John and explained the situation to him. He reached out to Cassie and the rest is history."

"Without asking me," I sigh. "I get that you have the means to do whatever you want. Thank you for trying to help, but I'm a big girl, I don't need you to save the day."

"White knight!" Layla yells from the couch.

I pinch the bridge of my nose. "Guys, could you not?"

"We flew to the other side of the country so you could be with the hot as fuck narrator who isn't even here," Amanda replies, sipping her wine. "I think that gives us the right to say whatever the hell we want in regards to your love life."

"I second that," Layla adds, raising her glass.

"Fine." I click the speaker button. "May as well make this a four-way conversation."

"Hi, Julian!" my friends say in unison.

Julian chuckles. "Don't unpack your bag. I'm headed to the airport right now. A driver will be at my house in fifteen minutes to pick you up and meet me at LAX."

"To go where? What did I say about throwing your money around?" I begin pacing again. My heart is racing. I don't know what to think about any of this.

"We need to get out of town for a few weeks, or a month, while the lawyers take care of everything."

"*We* don't need to go anywhere," I insist.

"Please, baby."

"Aww, the cute names have started," Layla coos.

I chew on my lip. "Maybe I should just go back to New York and let this blow over."

"Fuck that. You're going with the hot billionaire," Amanda says adamantly.

"If you want to go to New York, I'll arrange it. But... would you be okay if I came with you?" Julian asks. His voice is softer now, so full of hope.

I look up at the ceiling and take a deep breath. "Fine. Where do you want to take me?"

"Now that you've figured that out, can Layla and I crash here for a few weeks? I'm feeling my creative juices flowing being in a house the size of a small town," Amanda says, wiggling her eyebrows and biting her lip.

"Absolutely." Julian doesn't hesitate in his response. "Let me know if you need anything while you're there. You'll have to contend with the media out front, but otherwise, my place is yours until we return." I can hear Julian's smile through the phone. We have a lot to talk about, but for now, I'll allow myself to get wrapped up in my own billionaire romance.

"You know squatter's rights are a thing, right? I'm never leaving," Amanda says as she sits on the couch next to Layla. They clink their glasses.

"See you soon, my Becca. I love you." He hangs up.

"Asshole," I say to my phone, as if he could hear me.

"Have fun at your mystery destination, Becs." Layla smirks, now drinking straight from the wine bottle.

Amanda gives a knowing look, biting her lip. "Told you there would be a fuckfest."

# 35

# JULIAN

Everything is in motion and I'm now under contract with a new agent. I've received the manuscript for Harriet's book and will begin recording as soon as we return. Lawsuits are being drafted against Bryan and Andre. They might not stick, but I have to try.

The plane lands in Los Angeles and I rush to disembark, sprinting to the other terminal to meet Becca. The flight leaves in thirty minutes and has already started boarding. It'll take at least ten to get to the gate. I'm cutting it incredibly close.

I'll make it. I have to.

As I approach the gate, I open the app on my phone to get my ticket handy for the attendant. The waiting area is nearly empty, only a few people on their laptops who don't look like they're going anywhere anytime soon.

Becca is nowhere to be found.

*What if she changed her mind?*

*Please be on the plane.*

There's no one at the main kiosk to check her boarding status, so I scan my ticket and take a deep breath as I head down the ramp. I feel like my heart is in my throat. The attendants greet me as I step onto the plane. The moment of truth. I turn the corner and step into the aisle.

She's here.

I breathe a sigh of relief. It's as if my heart restarted the moment I saw her. Becca's looking out the window with earbuds in. She's dressed comfortably in sweatpants and a tee, wearing her hair up in a messy bun and my favorite purple rimmed glasses.

She spots me and does a double take, removing one of her earbuds.

*Time stops.*

I sit. I'm hesitant to do the one thing that feels natural, even as my palms itch to touch her. "My Becca," I whisper

She wets her lips, drawing my attention to them for a moment before I find her emerald eyes again. I tuck a stray lock of hair behind her ear, tracing her jaw as I begin to retract my hand.

*A zing courses through my body as I touch her.*

Her hand envelops mine, keeping it on her cheek.

*The air crackles between us and her breath hitches.*

She closes the distance and kisses me before I can do anything else. Her lips are soft and warm and make the world melt away. I love this woman more than I've ever loved anyone and, as impulsive as it is to feel this way about someone I met a month ago, I can't imagine kissing anyone else as long as I live.

A throat clears behind me, causing us to break apart far too quickly for my liking. "Sir. I'm sorry, but we'll need you to fasten your seatbelt. We're about to push off from the gate."

I buckle my seatbelt with lightning speed, turning back to Becca and putting my lips right back where they belong—on hers. She chuckles against me and I nip at her bottom lip in response. Her laugh quickly becomes a whimper as I pull away.

"I'm so sorry. For everything." I take her hand in mine, interlacing our fingers and bringing hers to my lips.

"You'll just have to make it up to me." She lifts her chin with confidence.

I kiss her neck and whisper against her skin, "We're actually going to see St. Tropez this time, but I also intend for my apology to extend into the bedroom—with my face between your legs."

She sucks in a breath. "Sounds like your typical Tuesday, not an apology," she says quietly, failing to keep her composure. I love that I have this effect on her. "But it's a good place to start."

"I love you." I kiss her once more before sitting back.

"You know, there's nowhere for you to go. You also can't hang up on me. I could sit here for the next several hours and torment you with all the horrible euphemisms for a vagina I can come up with. Or, I could just tell you I love you." She bites her lip, trying to hide her amusement.

"Do your worst, Merlot."

"I love you," she says, kissing my cheek.

I feign shock, gripping my heart with a gasp. Then, I laugh and wrap my arm around her. "I know, baby."

*If I have any say in the matter, I'm going to marry this beautiful stranger of mine.*

"We have a lot to talk about. But right now, can we not?"

"Whatever you want." I kiss the top of her head as she cuddles closer to me.

I've only been gone for a day, but it feels like a year. I already feel lighter with her beside me.

---

We're staying at the same resort but I reserved a larger room. We'll be here significantly longer than our last trip and I want to make sure we're comfortable. Part of me is intrigued by the idea of basically moving in together, albeit temporarily.

*Will the spell she has me under wear off once we're in close quarters?*

When we arrived at the resort, Becca wanted a few hours to write and she hasn't moved from the patio since. While she was typing away, I ran into town to pick up some essentials until we have time to do a full shopping for food and clothes. Her friend, Amanda, packed her duffle bag full of lacy underwear but only one pair of pants and shirt. Even though Becca will definitely need a full wardrobe, I should probably thank Amanda as soon as we get home.

*Home.*

When this is all over, I can't imagine going back to California while she's in New York. Wherever she is, I want to be there.

The sliding glass door is open, the coastal breeze seeping into the living space. I set the groceries on the counter and unload the perishables, leaving the rest for later. I picked up a dozen orange and pink roses, needing the nostalgia of when things weren't so fucked up. I unwrap them, clip the stems and put the "fuck me" flowers in water, chuckling to myself.

*No. She deserves better than "fuck me" flowers.*

I toss them in the trash and open a flower delivery site in my phone browser. I add two dozen red roses to the shopping cart.

*No, that screams proposal.*

*Delete.*

I type 'flowers that symbolize perfection' into my browser. It yields a few results, but I go with camellias and order a dozen to be delivered later today.

I cross the suite to the open patio door, leaning against the frame and taking in the view. The city is great, but it doesn't hold a candle to my girl. She's resting her arms on the railing, her hair whipping behind her. She looks so relaxed here. I know this audiobook situation has taken a toll on her and I hope this trip will give her the time and space to finish the book she's working on—a welcome distraction.

"Julian. I know you're lurking," she says, not looking at me.

"Hey, baby." I approach and wrap my arms around her middle, kissing her neck. She hums in response.

"That one's sticking, huh? *Baby* is the best you got," she replies, still admiring the city before us. I spot a small smirk tugging at the corner of her lips, but she quickly wipes it away by pressing her lips together.

"Fuck, I missed you."

I need her more than the oxygen in my lungs. I don't even need to be inside her, I just need her here in my arms for me to feel whole. I attempt to shake away the thought and fail miserably as she pushes her ass against me.

"Miss me? You were gone for, what, two hours?"

I sigh. "The last couple days have been absolute shit. Everything was amazing, and then it all fell apart."

Becca lets out a full laugh. I feel it everywhere. "Third act."

"What?"

"We're in our third act. Are you going to break up with me and come back groveling in two chapters?"

I chuckle and playfully bite her shoulder. "Smartass. You know there's no chance in hell I'd let you go. I never understood why the guys in romance books are such idiots."

"Um, news flash, you were, too. You signed a damn contract stating that you wouldn't see me for months."

"What's a few months?" I pull her closer. "The lawyers are taking care of it, but even if they can't find a work-around, it'll only be until the audiobook has been re-recorded. You think a piece of paper can keep me from you?"

"You're getting all growly," she sings.

"Oh, I'll show you growly."

# 36

## BECCA

Julian's fingers slip into my waistband, barely an inch. "Are you going to be my good girl and keep quiet while I play with your pussy?"

My voice comes out strangled. "Probably not."

His hand dips into my panties. A growl erupts from his chest, vibrating against me. "Already so wet for me. Spread your legs, baby. Attagirl, just like that." He pushes two fingers inside me, making me gasp. He pulls them out just as quickly, bringing them to his mouth. "Fuck, you taste so good."

Julian tugs down my pants and underwear in one swift movement. I step out of them and he tosses them onto the chaise lounge. I take off my glasses and throw them onto my pile of clothes. My breath is heavy with antici-pation as he slinks down with his back against the frosted pane glass.

"Get that pussy over here. I want you to make a mess all over my face." He hooks one of my legs over his shoulder and grabs my ass, pulling me to his mouth. The sounds of the city below us are drowned out by his groans against my clit as he sucks hard. *"Mine."*

A bark of a laugh escapes me. "You weren't kidding. Did you just growl 'mine' into my pussy?"

"Mmhmm." He sucks harder and pushes three fingers inside me, cutting off my laughter. "I need to stretch you out, baby. You're too tight."

"What man complains about a woman being too tight?"

He kisses my thigh and looks up at me. The look in his eyes is soft, full of both care and desire. "I never want to hurt you. When I fill you with my cock, I don't want it at the expense of your pleasure... Now, where was I?"

"You were making me come." I grip his hair and grind my pussy against his mouth. He chuckles against me. "Oh fuck. Do that again."

Julian hums against me and the sensation nearly pushes me over the edge. He continues slow, firm strokes on my clit as he moves his fingers in and out of me. I bite my lip in an attempt to stifle my moans. No one can see what he's doing to me but I don't want to draw attention to us, either.

"I'm close, don't stop... Right there... *Julian!*" I come hard, all at once not giving a shit who might've heard me.

"What did I say about being quiet, baby?"

"Oops."

He swiftly pulls his fingers out and rubs my sensitive clit. I gasp but it comes out as a full scream. My body is tingling all over as his touch prolongs my orgasm.

"I need your pussy wrapped around my cock. Or should I take one more from you with my mouth?"

"What kind of question is that? *No, don't lick my pussy, Julian.*" I roll my eyes. My sass backfires as he drives two of his fingers deep inside me.

"Maybe I shouldn't touch you for a week? Waiting until you're begging to come?"

I still. I went my entire life without having sex with this man, but the thought of him not touching me, even for a day, would be absolute torture. I knew he'd spoil me with that tongue of his.

"I would totally beg."

"Then you're going to give me one more before I fuck you so hard the whole damn country will hear me claim you as mine."

I swallow hard. "I thought you said you wanted me to be quiet?"

"What's the point? It's not like you listened the first time I asked." Julian pushes his fingers deeper. "Give me what's mine, baby." He circles his tongue around my clit, curling his fingers inside me, each time with more pressure. "Let me hear you."

"It's too much."

"You can take it." He slows his pace, but it's not what I

need. It's agonizingly slow, reminding me how desperately I ache to have him inside me.

"Faster," I breathe.

He gives me exactly what I need and, suddenly, I'm at the edge of my orgasm. It's so fucking close but I just can't quite get there. As if he can sense it, Julian removes his fingers and I pull my leg off his shoulder as he gets up. He stands behind me and kisses my shoulder.

"Open for me."

I do as he asks, spreading my legs and bending slightly as he pulls down his pants and boxer briefs. He teases his cock at my entrance and thrusts hard and deep inside me. I'm ready for him and welcome the added girth. Moving in and out of me slowly, he kisses my shoulder and neck. My grip on the rail tightens.

"Julian," I breathe.

"Fuck, you feel so good... *Fuck.*" He pulls out completely.

"What's wrong?" It takes me a moment to register: we always use condoms. "We can stop?" I offer. Julian doesn't respond, so I turn in his arms. "Really, it's okay." It makes so much sense why he'd be paranoid. Sixty billion dollars is a lot of money. I'm sure he's had some women... *bitches*... take advantage.

He kisses me and tasting me on his tongue unfortunately turns me on further. I'm left feeling empty and sexually frustrated.

"I'll run to the store real quick." I make a move to grab my pants, but he stops me.

"It's okay. I trust you."

"I don't mind, really. I know it's important to you."

Julian kisses me softly, his warm lips a welcome contrast to the cool breeze. When he pulls back, his eyes lock on mine. "Worst case, if you did get knocked up, I'd be tied to you indefinitely," he chuckles.

I huff out a laugh. "Not a chance. Sorry, if you have a breeding kink, it won't be satisfied tonight."

Julian kisses me again, smiling against my lips. He grabs my leg, hiking it up over his hip. "I don't but now that I've felt you without anything between us, I don't know that I can ever go back." He rubs his length against me before pushing inside.

I grip his back and thrust my hips against his, wanting him deeper. I can't get close enough.

"I love you," he says quietly, kissing my neck. "I want to come inside you. Is that okay?" he whispers, his hot breath causing goosebumps to erupt down my limbs and my nipples to tighten.

"Please," I whimper. His mouth crashes into mine. There is nothing gentle about how he's kissing me now. I'm being worshiped and claimed at the same time. "I... I love you, too," I mutter against his lips.

My back is pressed against the cold metal railing as he drives into me harder, but not faster. Having him bare is unlike anything I've ever experienced. Something about him feels different than the other times we've had sex. It's not just the lack of a condom. Something between us is now forever joined and there's no coming back from here. It's like each thrust isn't just bringing me closer to orgasm, he's showing me I'm his, as if we're two souls joining.

*No, this isn't a romance novel. He's not my soulmate. That doesn't exist.*

*Or does it?*

He thrusts harder and it only takes a minute before stars form behind my eyes. "I'm right there."

"Come for me, baby. Let go." Julian keeps the same pace and I shatter, selfishly not caring if he joined me . It feels too fucking good. Four more shallow thrusts and he comes too, settling inside me. He leans his forehead against mine. Our chests rise and fall in sync, as if we're one person.

"That was... I have no words for what that was."

"I know, baby. I know." He slowly pulls out of me. "You're fucking perfect. How are you feeling?" He tucks my wind swept hair behind my shoulders.

How *am* I feeling?

"Good." A vague answer is better than none.

"Let's get you cleaned up and then I have a surprise for you."

"If it involves your cock inside me, I don't know if I can handle it."

Julian chuckles. "No, it's better, I promise." He reaches between my legs and grazes my clit, making me shudder. "But I don't think I'll ever get enough of you, my Becca. Can I take another from you?"

"I thought we were going to play tourist this trip? Why do I feel like this is the beginning of a month-long fuck-fest, like Amanda predicted?"

"Okay." Julian removes his hand and I instantly miss his touch. "Let's go then." He steps back, pulls up his pants and heads inside.

"I was kidding!" My legs are jelly and I want to crumple to the floor, but I'll have to move if I want to chase after him.

He looks back at me, smiling. "Come on. I'm starving. We'll grab a bite to eat, then I'm going to spend the rest of the next day with my cock buried inside you," he says, gesturing with his head for me to join him. "We can be tourists tomorrow."

"I thought you were all about your appetizers," I counter.

"You're right." His hungry gaze drinks me in, landing on my still very naked bottom half. "On the bed. Now," he commands.

"Don't have to tell me twice, *my Julian*."

Julian waits at the doorway. I move past him with a light skip in my step, grazing his stomach as I pass. He doesn't wait for me to get on the bed, instead snaking his arm around my waist and pinning me against him. His other hand reaches up to claim the front of my throat, tilting my neck as he grazes his teeth against it.

"I know you narrate fantasy, but aren't you taking the vampire thing a little too far?"

He sucks hard on my neck, marking me. "You're mine, my Becca, just as I'm yours." I turn to face him, his hand never leaves my throat. "Now, be my good girl and lay down on the bed. I'm going to show you who that unnamed pussy really belongs to."

# 37

# JULIAN

"This is amazing!" Becca shouts through the aviation headset.

I can't wipe the smile off my face. I knew she'd love the helicopter tour; it allows her to see most of St. Tropez from above. The sun is setting, providing a magical backdrop for the city and its endless beaches.

"We'll need to head there in the morning." I point to Citadelle de Saint-Tropez. It looks almost like a small castle from the outside, but it's a maritime museum with incredible views.

"Should we picnic there like we're stuck in the 17th century?" she asks with a twinkle in her eyes.

"Absolutely." She could ask for anything and I'd give it to her.

After the tour, we go shopping for a dinner outfit; we can buy real clothes tomorrow. I found a great restaurant online that will give us an excuse to get dressed up.

In hindsight, I should've insisted that we grab her clothes before leaving; I'd love to see her in that black dress from the VIP party. She was absolutely breathtaking, but my cock also twitches at the memory of touching her that night.

Thankfully, there are several shops in town where she can pick a similar one if she wants. We check a few of them, not quite finding what she's looking for. She keeps insisting that she'd be happy grabbing a bite to eat at a cafe for a casual dinner, but I want to dote on her, spoil her, and take care of her. I want to give her the world. I have the means to do so—why shouldn't I?

We pull up to the restaurant and it's almost as beautiful as my date for the evening. Becca opted for a dark gray knee-length cocktail dress that accentuates her curves. There is no way in hell I'm keeping my hands to myself tonight, but being here, I don't have to. For the past month, after all the sneaking around, it's as if a weight has been lifted off me since we left the States. I can be present with her without worrying about who might see us.

Our table overlooks the water that's illuminated only by moonlight. If I ever proposed, it would be right here. Hell, I'd marry her tonight if she said yes.

*Fuck, what am I saying?*

I can definitely see myself marrying her one day, but it would probably scare the shit out of her if I mentioned spending forever with her, right now.

"Okay, I know these are supposed to go in a particular

order, but if I want cheese first? Can't I just have it first?"

I chuckle, shaking my head. "Do you want us to get kicked out?"

"I know. I've seen enough food shows to know that it would basically be sacrilegious. But did you see that plate?" She nods her head toward the table next to us.

"Good things come to those who wait," I reply, lightly licking my lips. As I do, her gaze falls to them and her breath catches. She composes herself quickly but she can't hide the fire in her eyes.

The five-course meal includes wine pairings. The waiter pours two glasses of a sauvignon blanc that's less crisp than I'm used to. Becca takes a sip and lets out a satisfied hum.

This is what I want. I want all of her, of course, but I can't seem to get enough of this part of her that's lighter, freer. I love seeing her so relaxed and enjoying herself.

Our first course arrives and, as the waiter leaves, my phone chimes in my pocket with a notification I use for my front gate. "Shit, sorry. I thought I turned that off." I reach into my pocket to switch my phone over to vibrate. It buzzes once. Twice. The third time, I'm ready to throw it into the ocean.

"Whoever it is, they really want to talk to you. Step out and take the call. I don't mind. But just know that I'm going to dive into dinner without you," she says with a wink.

"Are you sure?" I get up and lean in to kiss her. She nods. "I'll be quick." With her friends at my house, I need to make sure everything is okay.

My phone continues to vibrate as I exit the restaurant. I pull up the first video. "Hey, baby, it's me. Are you home?"

*Katrina. Fuck.*

Why the fuck is she at my house? I click on the next video.

"Open up, or I'll tell these guys with cameras about all the dirty things you want to do to me."

Third video.

"Julian. What the fuck? I know you're home. Your staff's cars are all here. I know you're back from New York."

"Bitch, stop ringing the doorbell! Julian isn't here." Amanda's voice comes from Katrina's right but out of view.

"Who the fuck are you?" Katrina asks, crossing her arms.

"Who the fuck are *you?*" Amanda counters.

"I'm his girlfriend, and—"

I refresh my phone but there are no new videos, and with the last one cut off, I'm incredibly anxious. Layla and Amanda should still be at the house, so I access the intercom system to call them.

"Amanda? Layla? Are you guys still there?"

There's a pause, causing my heart rate to spike. Layla finally answers, "Hey. Yeah, I'm here.

"Amanda is out front dealing with your *girlfriend*."

"I can explain. She's not my—"

"Oh, I know. Don't get your panties in a twist, I'm just fucking with you. We know you don't have some mystery girlfriend on the side. You know, you're lucky we're romance authors and can spot a miscommunication trope from a mile away. Amanda's sending her packing right now."

I let out a sigh of relief. "So, everything's okay? Do you need me to call the cops or anything?"

"Everything's fine. Well, except one thing: your personal chef is hot as hell, but he's gay. Can you hire a straight one so I can live out my fantasy of running off into the sunset with a man who'll cook for me?"

I laugh, running my hand through my hair. "I'll see what I can do."

"Well, get back to your fuckfest. We have everything handled here." She hangs up without a goodbye. I pocket my phone and walk back into the restaurant.

As I approach the table, Becca is laughing at something on her phone. I carefully place my hand on her back, not wanting to startle her.

"Sorry about that." I kiss her temple and take my seat, placing the napkin on my lap.

"So, it sounds like the girls are having entirely too much

fun at your place." She puts her phone away and wiggles her eyebrows.

"Yeah. I just talked to Layla. My ex showed up."

"Oh, you mean your *girlfriend?* Was she hoping to rekindle the flame and make up in the last few chapters, or is she the villain showing up to break up the happy couple?" She takes a sip of wine in an attempt to hide her smile.

"All of the above." I shrug. "How are you so cool about this? When I saw Bryan was on that panel with you..." I shake my head. "We weren't even dating, but I felt this overwhelming urge to, I don't know, break his kneecaps."

Becca laughs. "You should've. Just make sure you get it on video so I can watch it on repeat."

"Why were you with him?" I take a hearty spoonful of my tomato gazpacho and bring it to my lips, not breaking eye contact with her.

She blows out a long breath. "That's a loaded question. He was charming and made me feel like I was his whole world. I was wrapped up in him. Sound familiar?" While she says it in jest, her words hurt. An ache fills my heart at being compared to him.

"You think that's what this is?"

"Yes... No... I mean, maybe? I don't think you're anything like him. I fell hard and fast for him, but it was nothing like this. To be honest, I don't know what the hell this is, but it's scary, and wonderful, and unexpected, and most days it feels unreal. So, no, this isn't like with

Bryan. You're significantly more charming." She smiles, biting her lip.

I'm about to ask what happened between them when the waiter approaches with our next course: a caprese salad with pinot grigio wine pairing. I take a few bites of my salad but notice Becca moves a piece of balsamic-glazed mozzarella around on her plate, lost in thought.

I avoid the dreaded question of asking how it ends, not wanting to ruin our dinner. "He was a fucking idiot. But I guess I should thank him for making the biggest mistake of his life. We could've never met."

"You know, I wasn't supposed to sit next to you on the plane. I had a discounted upgrade offer for first class. I almost didn't take it, but decided to treat myself." She takes her first bite of her salad.

"Really? I wasn't supposed to be on that flight, either. I hit traffic coming into LA and missed my flight. I was able to get a seat on that one, just had to wait a few hours." Becca offers me a small smile. "A series of fortunate events."

"Would make a good title for the book I'm writing."

"Are you going to tell me what it's about?"

"Nope. You'll just have to buy it when it comes out." The twinkle in her eyes is back.

"I'll be first in line with highlighters in hand."

"So, I aired out my dirty laundry. Why is a beautiful woman showing up at your house looking for love? I promise, I won't put it in a book. My friends, on the other hand? I can't guarantee they won't."

My face falls. I know we should talk about it, but talking about another woman with Becca just feels wrong. "I was going to marry her."

She stills, fork halfway to her mouth. "Oh." She sets it down and takes a long drink of her wine.

"I had a weekend getaway planned. I was going to take her to Seattle and do a cliché Space Needle proposal. I got home from recording early to pack and found Katrina in bed with another guy."

"You lived together?"

"No." I don't elaborate, but she looks at me expectantly, so I say simply, "I was only proposing because it felt like the next right step."

"Was she," Becca clears her throat and gulps, lowering her voice, "*your* Katrina?"

I chuckle. "No, baby. Not a chance. I never really called her anything other than Kat. That's it." I shouldn't enjoy her slight jealousy, but I do. I would never do anything to make her feel that way on purpose, but I love that she cares. "There was no turbulence, *my Becca*. I've been yours since we met."

"There was turbulence," she insists but her smile and that twinkle in her eyes gives her away.

"No." I shake my head. "You, my beautiful stranger, are just trying to be a voice of reason when we both know that this, you and me, was always supposed to happen."

"Fated mates, huh?"

"I don't care how ridiculous it sounds. There's no logical explanation for how I feel about you. You're stuck with me. It was written in the stars," I tease.

Becca looks out to the moonlit water then back to me with a beaming smile. "Maybe you're right."

I'm going to marry this woman and spend the rest of my life doing whatever it takes to keep that beautiful smile on her face.

# 38

# BECCA

*One Month Later*

"Do we have to go back?" I whine.

"If I had any say in it, we'd never leave." Julian kisses my temple. The airport bustling around us fades away as I cuddle closer to him.

*Now boarding group one for flight 8374 to New York JFK.*

I swallow my tears.

"That's us, baby." Julian squeezes my hand tightly and guides us to the attendant scanning tickets.

This month has been absolutely incredible. We stayed off the grid as much as possible, just enjoying our time together. We spent our days on the beach or exploring the city. I finished my book, we visited Nice, and even managed a weekend trip to Milan. Our nights were spent making love and falling asleep wrapped in each other's arms. There's no other way to describe it, it's definitely not sex.

The only hiccup: we have to spend the next month apart. I have a book tour with the re-release of *Delivery of Fate* that Cassie signed me up for. Julian has to record an audiobook for an up-and-coming YA fantasy author. Unfortunately, the contract Julian signed with Andre is in full effect and we can't be seen together for the next twenty-six days... and counting. This flight is the last I'll see of him and I want to savor every minute.

Nine short hours later, we land in New York. My heart is heavy, knowing I have to say goodbye to him. We disembark and, as we enter the terminal, two high pitched squeals come from the waiting area. "Becca!"

"What are you doing here?" I wrap Amanda and Layla in a tight hug.

"Your billionaire boyfriend flew us in," Layla says laughing.

We break apart. Julian's arm snakes around my waist, pulling me to him. He's been over-the-top affectionate since our days were numbered in St. Tropez. He kisses my shoulder and Amanda rolls her eyes at the innocent PDA.

"My flight leaves in forty minutes." Julian's voice lacks his usual flair; it's melancholy. "It's in another terminal, so I need to get going."

I turn in his arms, my heart suddenly feeling heavier. "I can walk with you."

"No," he says softly. "I don't want it to be any harder than it already is." Lifting my chin with his thumb and forefinger, he kisses me.

Tears prick behind my eyes. I feel like I've found the love of my life and he's being taken from me. It's only twenty-fucking-six days, but after spending the last month together, I can't imagine a single day without him.

"I love you, my Becca," he whispers against my lips.

"I—" He kisses me harder, his tongue dancing with mine so I can't get the words out.

Amanda's throat clears behind me. "Okay, guys. It's a few weeks. Keep it in your pants."

"Twenty-six days," he mutters against my lips before pulling back.

"Okay, but all it would take is a random ass person walking by to snap a photo of you two, and you'll be in hot water," Layla reminds us gently.

Julian kisses me one last time. "I'll call you when I land." He slings his bag over his shoulder, walks away for a few steps but returns, gripping the back of my neck and kissing me one last time. "Okay, I'm going, I promise."

I call after him, "I love you!"

He turns with a smirk. "Not as much as I love you, my Becca."

I watch him walk away. Layla wraps her arms around me to my right and Amanda holds my hand to my left. As soon as he's out of view, I let my tears fall. I've never loved anyone or anything as much as I love Julian. My heart is broken in two knowing I can't be with him right now.

What are the chances that I met the love of my life? Not just someone I care deeply about, but over-the-top consuming love? Once in a lifetime love? Fated mates love?

I can't stay in New York. Not permanently. Not when he's in California and a piece of my heart is headed there.

"There, there," Amanda pats my shoulder. I know she writes deliciously angsty love in her books but there's a good chance I'm making her uncomfortable with my theatrics.

I take a long, deep breath. "Okay, let's get home."

"Uh... I don't live here," Layla says with wide eyes.

Amanda and I laugh. I offer, "My place is your place, as long as you like."

We leave the terminal, head to baggage claim, and grab a rideshare. I welcome the change from having a personal driver, and helicopter rides, and private planes, and fancy restaurants, and... *Julian.* I don't care about that life. I only want him.

"All right, babe, let's get you home. You stink after that trip across the pond," Amanda says, sarcastically pinching her nose.

*Home.*

My apartment. I haven't seen it in a month. Mrs. Goldstein agreed to look after it, but I trust that as much as I trust Daddy to not hide under a bed.

"I need to move," I say mostly to myself, but both of them look at me as if I told them I was joining a cult. "I can't stay here when he's in California."

"You gonna grand gesture this shit?" Amanda asks.

I shrug. "I mean, maybe I should."

———

Twelve days. Twelve fucking days. How I made it this long is beyond me. I'm more determined than ever to move. I put my apartment up for sale, but there've been no bites. I'm closing on a small house in Lake Elsinore in a cash sale and am getting the hell out of the tri-state area and into the sauna that's Southern California.

I don't expect to move in with Julian, but living anywhere near his mansion of a house isn't in my budget. The best I can do is a lake town thirty minutes away. Southern California can get incredibly hot and I need to be near water; I'm not sure I can handle the heat.

"I can't believe you're leaving," Amanda says solemnly, helping me pack and stack boxes. "We're New Yorkers."

"I'll come visit. My agent and editor are here... and you."

I have two weeks until I can openly be with him without any sort of breach of contract. Two weeks of hell in a lake city I don't know. My *boyfriend* thought it was a good idea to put up millions of dollars for sake of my literary reputation. Asshole. Sweet in theory, but I'd trade all the fame from my books if it meant I didn't have to be away from Julian.

Maybe I should buy a boat? My advance on my new book might cover it.

I should get a fucking boat.

I can look up videos online on how to drive it, store it, and winterize it. Apparently, that's a thing.

This can be my life now.

Boat life.

"Becs? You okay?"

Amanda's voice pulls me from my daydream. "Sure, yeah. I'm fine."

"Don't buy a boat," she says with a side eye.

*Shit, I thought that was all internal dialogue.*

"What else am I supposed to do in a lake town?"

"Oh, I don't know, fuck Julian?"

I snicker. "Oh, I will, but I can't for two weeks."

Amanda sighs and takes out her phone. She types for entirely too long. "Vibrator will be delivered to your new address tomorrow."

"What?" I shriek.

"Where is the miscommunication? Vibrator. Delivered to your new place. Tomorrow." She shows me her phone for proof.

I pinch the bridge of my nose. "Really?"

"Should I get Layla on this? She looks all sweet and innocent but you know damn well you'll end up with some giant dildo arriving at your door. Girl writes fantasy-ish, I trust her vibrator game zero percent. Monster dongs will be coming your way."

"I don't need my clit to fall off."

Amanda agrees, "Yeah, so accept my early house-warming and be done with it."

"What if I fucked this all up and, after the last few weeks, he's decided he doesn't love me anymore?"

I haven't even texted Julian since we landed at JFK. I've been too paranoid. He called me when he landed and sent me a burner phone, like I'm some kind of mafia princess or drug dealer. *Maybe I should write a mafia romance next?*

Other than my checking the charge on the incredibly expensive, latest model, burner phone, I haven't looked to see if he's called. I have no way of reaching him. He deleted his social media, so I can't even stalk him like a crazy ex.

Amanda gets up and heads into the kitchen, pulling over one of the four vases of obscenely large rose bouquets. "If these aren't "fuck me" flowers, I don't know what is."

"It's not like that." *Okay, maybe it is.* "It's not like he's going to—"

There's a knock at the door and Amanda and I exchange a confused look. I sprint for it, throwing my door open. "Juli— *Bryan.*"

"Hey, kitten."

# 39

# JULIAN

I can't live without her. I know it's risky but after almost two weeks of hiding from the media and Becca, I need to see her. I look ridiculous in a dark gray hoodie and sunglasses, but it's worth it if I get to see my girl.

I take the steps two at a time.

"Hey, kitten."

I still, seven steps before I reach her landing.

*No. There's no fucking way.*

"What the fuck do you want?" Becca spits.

*Ok, so this wasn't a planned thing.*

"Can I come in?"

"Fuck no, you can't." Amanda's voice comes from inside the apartment. "Take one step and I'll have her boyfriend here faster than a fucking roadrunner."

"Wait, you have his number?" Becca says to her, barely above a whisper.

"Shut up, you suck at this," Amanda replies. I have to keep myself from laughing.

Becca giggles for a moment then clears her throat. "Right. What are you doing here?"

"Brenda left me, with just dinner and a note."

"Aw, so sad... Fuck off, North," Amanda says with a shit ton of gusto. I take note not to ever upset Becca or I'll be dealing with Amanda.

"Can I come in?" Bryan asks. "That asshole Julian took everything from me. And that Barlowe bitch sued me and Andre, and now I'm left with—"

"I'm sorry," Becca interrupts, her voice laced with sarcasm. "What did you think was going to happen when you sabotaged my audiobook? You and Andre both got what you deserved."

Bryan is quiet for a moment. Then, says softly, "I want you back, kitten."

"Absolutely not," Becca bites. "You aren't invited and you have shit timing. I'm moving to California."

*Wait, what?*

"California? Why? Brenda and I are over. I thought maybe we could pick up where we left off?"

"Fuck you. Fuck Brenda. Stay the hell away from my friend, Bryan." Amanda's voice lowers as she continues,

"There are too many B's here, Becs." She raises it again. "Bryan, if you don't leave, I'll take care of you worse than I did Katrina."

"Who's Katrina?" Bryan asks

"I said fuck off, or I'll—"

There's a crunch, followed by a "what the fuck?" coming from Bryan.

"You thought I was joking?" Amanda snickers. "I was waiting for the moment you crossed her threshold to knock your ass out. Want to call the cops? I'm sure her sweet neighbor with the oddly named cat would be more than happy to vouch for me."

I don't need to step in and handle Becca's battles. She has it covered. If she doesn't, she has a few incredibly strong-willed friends who have no issue throwing a punch. I make my way down the stairs to the floor below hers, awaiting Bryan's inevitable departure. Thankfully, only a couple minutes pass before he runs past me with his tail between his legs.

I slowly make my way back up the stairs. I knock four times and Amanda opens the door.

"What did I—" She breaks off mid-sentence and smiles. "What did I say about grand gestures?"

Becca groans and approaches the door. "Now what does he— *Julian?*"

"I'll leave you to it," Amanda tells me with a wink.

The moment she leaves, Becca slaps me. Full on, palm

across the face. My hand instinctively rubs it, relishing the sting. I fucking deserve it for disappearing.

"Where the fuck have you been?" She crosses her arms over her chest.

"I have some good news." I try to hold in my excitement, already moving past the sting of her slap.

Becca's shoulders fall. "What good news? I had an asshole at my door a minute ago, I'm trying to pack to— *spoiler*—surprise you in California, and—"

I close the distance, wrap her in my arms, and bring her lips to mine. I kiss the hell out of her without caution. I missed her too fucking much to not touch her, not kiss her, not feel her in my arms like she's mine.

"You're moving to California?" I ask against her lips. She nods and kisses me back with a ferocity I haven't felt in weeks. While it's a risk, being here with her feels... right.

"Lake Elsinore," Becca replies but then pulls back. "What the hell are you doing here?" She looks behind me. "Did anyone see you?"

"Why are you moving to California?"

"Are you that fucking dense? I was coming for you. I bought a place thirty minutes from you," Becca groans. "It was supposed to be a surprise."

"Not much of a surprise when your apartment went up for sale," I challenge.

"There haven't been any bids, but there was someone

interested yester— *you*. Was it you? Why? Why would you want a tiny apartment in the Upper East Side?"

I wrap her in my arms. "Yes, it was me. I had to come back for you."

Becca laughs, resting her forehead against my chest and fisting my shirt. She whispers, "You came for me."

I glide my hand into her hair, stroking her cheek with my thumb and pulling her emerald gaze to mine. "There is nothing I wouldn't do for you, my Becca. You're here, so I am, too."

"I love you," she whispers.

"Not as much as I love you, baby. So, tell me, where do you want to live?"

She shakes her head. "I don't care. As long as there's air conditioning and internet, I want to be where you are."

"Move in with me." The words slip from me before I can stop them.

"Yes, she says yes!" Amanda yells from the living room.

Becca looks back to her. "Shh! You're ruining his third act moment." She turns back to me. "Amanda's right. I'll move in with you. On one condition."

"You and your conditions." A wide grin spreads across my face. "Name it, and it's yours."

"We buy a new place together that isn't a fucking castle."

"Always the voice of reason, my Becca." I kiss her softly. "Anything else?"

"Yes. Can you hire movers? This shit is a pain in the ass. You want your girl to move in with you, gotta pay the price. Oh, and best friends are included. You're stuck with my friends too, expect them to drop by frequently."

"That's right, you tell him," Amanda chimes in.

Becca and I both laugh but it's cut short when I tell her, "I didn't tell you my surprise."

"I thought you being here was my surprise?"

"They reworked the contract. I no longer have a clause that keeps me from seeing the woman I love." I pull her closer by the small of her back and her breath catches.

"So, you can kiss me in public?"

I bite my lip, unable to hide my smile. "As of tomorrow? Yeah."

"I love you." Becca doesn't let me respond. Her lips are on mine in an instant. I kiss her back harder, relishing the feel of her body pressed against mine. It's only been a couple weeks—twelve days to be exact—but it feels like months, years even. I'm a starved man; I can't get enough of her.

She walks us into her apartment, her lips never breaking from mine. Amanda slides out, without a word, and I can't help but chuckle at her stealthy behavior.

"I love you, my Becca," I finally reply.

"See. Now you know how it feels being cut off." She pauses for a moment. "There's just one thing."

"What's that, baby?"

"Daddy."

"Huh?" I ask with a laugh.

"It's not just the name of my neighbor's cat."

"Okay?"

"It's also the name of my..."

# EPILOGUE
## BECCA

*One Year Later*

"Thank you, again, for agreeing to the book tour. *A Series of Fortunate Events* has to be my favorite book I've read this year." Emma continues helping me pack my collateral materials. This is the fourth sold out book signing, we're leaving with only a small box of stickers and bookmarks.

Emma was so amazing at helping Julian get out from under Andre's thumb a year ago, the least I can do is make an appearance at a few book signings to promote a few of her authors.

"The pleasure is mine. How's Harriet's next book coming along?"

"Great! I'm still trying to convince her to traditionally publish. Her book is so amazing, I want to see it widely distributed. But, she insists on staying indie."

I chuckle. "Can you blame her?"

"This is all *your* doing, you know." Emma wags her finger at me.

"I know, I know." I raise my hands in surrender. "I just couldn't risk working with someone like Andre or Bryan again."

"I don't blame you. Those guys were assholes."

"That's putting it mildly," I say with a scoff.

"Are you sure you don't want to sign with me?"

"Maybe one day, but for now, I'm enjoying the freedom of being independently published again."

"Hey, baby." Julian appears behind me, wrapping his arms around my torso. He kisses my temple and I melt into his embrace. "Ready to head out?"

"Yep." I turn in his arms. "Just the one small box today."

Julian's grin spreads from ear to ear. "You sold out again, didn't you?" I nod. "So fucking proud of you." I lift onto my toes and kiss him. He pulls me closer and glides his hand into my hair, forcing a moan from me.

Emma clears her throat. "Okay, lovebirds. Get out of here. You're fogging up the glass."

"You're one to talk," Julian replies with a chuckle. "Don't act all innocent. I've seen you with that Dylan of yours."

Emma blushes. "That's different."

"You know, I'd love to tell your story sometime. Names changed to protect the not so innocent, of course," I say, raising an eyebrow. Her love story beats mine by a long shot and second chance romance is hot right now. I shouldn't write to market, but for Emma's story, I totally would.

She rolls her eyes. "He'd never allow it. Well, I'm headed out. If you need anything before the next signing, let me know!"

Emma grabs a box and heads out of the bookstore. Julian leans in and whispers, "Your bag is packed and in the car. Come have an adventure with me."

I gasp, "Where are we going?"

"Just a little trip. Don't worry, I had Amanda pack your bag for you," he says with a wink.

"Fuck. It's all thongs, isn't it?"

Julian shrugs. "Guess we'll just have to find out."

---

"Is your document saved?" Julian's voice pulls me from my draft as he sits next to me on the chaise lounge. Our hotel room overlooks the water, reminding me of our month-long trip to St. Tropez a year ago. The sunny beaches of Miami have been the perfect backdrop for writing. If I can't be in St. Tropez for inspiration, Florida's clear blue waters are a perfect substitute.

I quickly double check my computer and sigh in relief. "Yes. Fuck. Don't scare me like that."

He leans over me, shuts my laptop, and closes the

distance. He doesn't kiss me, stopping less than an inch from my lips. "Can you take a break?"

I'll never get used to him calling me that—it still gives me butterflies. "Yeah, I just got to the good part, but I can take a break." I set my laptop on the side table and hook my hand behind his neck, pulling him to me. He chuckles against my lips.

"What were you writing?" he asks as he trails kisses down my neck.

"I... uh... it doesn't matter."

Julian pulls back. "I can't wait any longer."

"Oh?" My eyebrows raise. "Do I have to be quiet? I don't think the beach goers will be too thrilled to hear me moaning 'Julian.' The waves might drown out some of it, though."

A hearty laugh comes from his chest. "No, baby." He reaches into his pocket, pulling out a jewelry box. My heart leaps into my throat as my hand flies to my mouth.

He opens it. It's a beautiful emerald cut solitaire in white gold. Simple and elegant. "Julian," I breathe.

"Will you make me the happiest man alive and marry me, my Becca?"

I wrap my arms around his neck, nodding frantically. "Fuck, it took you long enough." He holds me tighter and kisses my shoulder and neck. "Yes, of course I'll marry you."

He removes the ring from the box. "I've had this ring for a year. I bought it in St. Tropez. I would've asked you sooner but I had a surprise planned for you." He slides it onto my finger.

"Here I thought we were going to have balcony sex. This is so much better." I cup his cheek and kiss him softly.

"I love you," he whispers against my lips.

"Not as much as I love you, *my Julian,*" I tease.

"I suppose I can tell you your surprise now."

"What now?" I pull back, frowning. "You've already given me my perfect epilogue ending." Julian pulls out his phone, showing me his airline app.

"St. Tropez? Then why the hell are we in Miami?" I can't wipe the smile from my face.

"Had to throw you off my scent. I don't want to wait to marry you. I had Ethan arrange everything. I want you to be my wife tomorrow... Unless that's too soon?" His voice shakes at his question.

"Get married in St. Tropez? On one condition." I bite my lip. His smile returns.

"Whatever you want."

"I'm not waiting for the end of the meal; I want cheese as an appetizer." Whoever made up that rule about cheese not being an appetizer in France should live in Tartarus.

"If it means I get to spend the rest of my life with you, consider it done, my Becca."

## LOVED A VOICE WITHOUT REASON?

I hope you loved reading Becca and Julian's story as much as I loved writing it!

Wherever you feel most comfortable, please consider leaving a review on Goodreads, Amazon, or social media! Your honest review means the world to me.

While this book is part of the Love at All Cost series, you may have noticed cameos from the Top Shelf Romances. Keep reading for a two chapter sneak peek of *Mine with Extra Lime* to find out how Emma and Dylan met.

Don't worry, you'll see more of Becca, Layla, and Amanda in *Not Her Villain* and *Unexpectedly Ruined*!

To keep up with all of my upcoming releases, be sure to follow me over on Amazon!

xoxo,
Irene

# MINE WITH EXTRA LIME
## SNEAK PEEK

# CHAPTER 1

## EMMA

"Is this your first mixer?" I can't fault my new boss, Susan, for trying to gauge exactly how much marketing experience I have. I'm only twenty-one, and while I didn't embellish my resumé, my experience is more in management than marketing or sales—definitely not networking.

"Oh, no, this isn't my first," I lie as our car approaches the mixer where I'm likely not qualified to represent her company.

As I step out of the car, I become increasingly nervous. *What am I doing? I don't know how to network!* Luckily, another account executive, Katie, is already here to hold my hand through it.

She meets us at the car and whispers, "You've got this, Emma," as she links her arm with mine. "Just walk in, grab a glass of wine, and keep to yourself this round. The goal is to get to know everyone. People want to do business with someone they like and they're going to *love* you! Watch what Susan and I do, and you'll be fine."

I blow out a deep breath, only to stop dead in my tracks as we cross the threshold into the mixer. *Is everyone here over sixty-five?* Katie squeezes my arm once before heading to the open bar across the room. I follow a few steps behind her and pick up a glass of whatever wine is being served. After a quick taste, I'm sure the varietal is just "white wine." While I'm no connoisseur, this is definitely something that came from a box. I should be careful; I don't want to be hungover tomorrow from a glass of cheap chardonnay.

Katie wanders over to one of our existing clients, who gives her a tight hug, then with a warm smile shakes the hand of the person next to them.

*Man, she's good at this.*

Sipping my sad excuse for wine, I scan the room. After a minute of not recognizing anyone I recognize from the chamber of commerce listings, I spot a gorgeous, tall man with dark hair and glasses. He can't be older than twenty-five, making us two of the youngest people here. I have absolutely no game when it comes to men, but I do know that I should *not* be staring at him for more than a few seconds, especially since he hasn't taken his eyes off me.

I tear my eyes from the stranger, searching for Susan or Katie, finding they're both entertaining other attendees. I make my way to Katie, hoping for an opportunity to learn from her. Meanwhile, I can still feel the mystery man's eyes on me. It's making my heart race and stomach flip.

I sneak a quick glance to see if he's still looking my way. He absolutely is. My cheeks are warm, and I can try to convince myself it's from the wine, but it's from the attention of the most attractive man I've ever seen. His ability to make my breath hitch from a single glance is too much to handle at a professional event.

*Get it together, Emma!*

Our gazes meet again, and I need to find out who the hell this guy is. As I reach Katie, I interrupt as professionally as I can, "So sorry, can I steal Katie away for a few moments?" She looks at me with intrigue, and as we walk away after excusing ourselves, I lean in and whisper, "Hey, who's that guy over there?"

She looks to our left. "The younger one with glasses?" I nod. "I don't know. I haven't seen him before, but *damn*, he can't take his eyes off you! Shoot, I wish I had a guy who looked at me like that."

I double check as stealthily as I can, and his intense gaze is still focused our way, sipping his drink. He's hardly paying attention to the men he's standing with.

"Go introduce yourself! You're single and he's checking you out like he's moments away from finding a dark corner and having his way with you."

"I could *never!* That's way too forward. Plus, we're here for work," I insist. I consider walk over to the bar to escape this whole thing, but remain rooted in place when notice he's excusing himself from the two men he's talking to and heading in the same direction.

*So much for escaping.*

"Oh my God, Emma! Yes, you can. Wait, it looks like he might beat you to it. Quick, tell me something funny." Katie's eyes are twinkling with delight, which only makes me more nervous. I'm pretty sure I've become her entertainment for the mixer; no good can come from this.

"Katie, what the heck? I'm not funny, and what do you mean he might beat me to—"

I feel his presence like an electric charge filling the air before I hear him. "Hi there. Hope I'm not interrupting?" His voice is low, practically a purr, and shiver runs up my spine as I turn around.

"Oh, hi. Um, of course not! We were just, uh... talking shop."

*Who the hell says "talking shop?" Come on, Emma, do better! Focus...*

How can I, though? He's one of the most beautiful men I've ever met with the most adorable dimpled smile, dark blue eyes that pierce my soul, and I'm wrapped in his scent of leather and embers. *Or maybe that's just the name of the candle that I bought on my last Target run?* I blow out a deep breath; it's criminal how attractive this man is.

*Oh, shit, how long have I been staring?*

I'm pulled from my thoughts as he hands Katie and me a glass of wine. "I noticed you both were running low."

Katie declines, "Oh, I don't accept drinks from anyone other than a bartender, *but* I am Emma's ride, so she can have mine. I have to make sure she gets home safe."

I smack her arm and turn back to him. "I… yeah, sure, thanks." I'm unable to get the words out as he pours one glass into the other and hands it to me. As I take it, our fingers brush. An innocent touch, but it causes goose-bumps to erupt all over my body.

*Does he feel that too? I sure as hell did.*

"I don't think we've been properly introduced," I announce with as much confidence as I can muster. "I'm Emma, and this is Katie. We work for a local magazine."

He holds out his hand and I take it. *There's that zing again.* "Dylan. It's a pleasure to meet you, Emma. I haven't seen you here before, is this your first time?" His lack of acknowledgement of Katie isn't lost on me—all his focus is on me.

"Yes, but Katie has been before." His eyes never leave mine, even at the second mention of my coworker. The energy in the room is heavy; I don't know what it is about this guy, but I feel a pull toward him and can't look away.

Katie clears her throat, likely uncomfortable with what-ever *this* is. "Okay, right, so I need to check on a few people. It was great to meet you, Dusty."

"Dylan," he corrects.

"Right, Dylan. Emma, I'll find you later." She winks at

me and I wince in embarrassment. Hopefully he didn't catch it.

*Who the hell winks at people?*

"I'm sorry, she's... well, that's Katie," I admit sheepishly. I'm not sure what to say, but I desperately need to fill the silence. "So, Dylan, what brings you here tonight? What do you do?"

He brings his drink to his lips and his gaze hasn't wavered once, remaining on me like we're the only two people in the room. "Investments."

*That could mean literally anything, could he be any more vague?*

Dylan takes out a card from his wallet and hands it to me. "My personal number is on the bottom. It was great to meet you, Emma." Disappointment stabs me in the gut as he walks away, glancing over his shoulder with a dimpled grin. Brushing off the interaction as purely professional, I place the card in my purse, and set down my too-full glass of wine to find Katie. I need to get the hell out of here before my cheeks get any redder.

"So, how did it go?" Katie teases. "Did he ask you out?"

"I don't want to talk about it." He's easily the most handsome man I have ever met, but it's more than that; I feel a gravitational pull toward him that I can't explain. Except, I may have imagined it all.

---

The next day as I arrive at the office, Katie greets me at the door with two cups of coffee. Bouncing with excitement, she hands me one and asks, "Did you call him? Did he call you?"

I set the coffee on my desk, shrug off my coat, and take a seat. Powering up my computer, I sigh, "No, I didn't call him. We just met *last night.*"

She eyes me suspiciously, sipping her own drink. "Call him *now!* What are you waiting for?"

What *am* I waiting for? I can easily call his work number under the guise of a business call. I hate that it's dishonest, and what would I even say? *"Hi, it's Emma, we spoke for like 2.5 seconds and I think you're incredibly attractive. Want to hang out sometime?""*

Instead, I tell her, "Maybe tomorrow, I need to catch up on emails." Focusing on my computer to avoid her gaze and persistent matchmaking, I check my schedule for the day. "I have a luncheon *and* another mixer today?"

Katie doesn't even blink. "Yep, and Susan wants you to go to both."

"Seriously?" I sigh and bring my coffee to my lips for the first time, forgetting that Katie takes her coffee black. I wince at the bitterness and set it down. "Fine, I'll go, but only because there's a full bar at this one."

Katie laughs and leaves my office while I dive into work for a few hours.

---

At tonight's mixer, there's a much younger crowd. Susan sent Katie and me alone this time, but since I'm still learning the ropes, I really have no business being here without her.

We grab a few glasses of white wine right after we arrive. Unfortunately, the advertised full bar is all well liquor. I don't need to be praying to the porcelain gods because of a bottom shelf gin and tonic.

"He's here," Katie whisper-shouts.

"Who?" I scan the room. Just as I'm about to turn back to her, I spot Dylan. He's laughing with a few older gentlemen and a woman. Thankfully, I don't think he's seen me yet, and I can hide in the sea of people between us. "Oh, Dylan? It makes sense. He is here to network, just like us."

"Oh, come on! This is such a cliché meet cute." Katie is way too invested in this.

"You've read too many romance novels. This is *not* a meet cute. This is not destiny, or happenstance... or whatever the hell you want to label it." I roll my eyes at her and sip my wine, which is, surprisingly, better than last night. "Who are our prospects tonight; who does Susan want us to meet?"

"You can start with Mr. McHottie over there," she jokes, gesturing to Dylan. Just as I'm about to open my mouth to protest, he looks our way. "Looks like we've been spotted, Em. Okay, so I'm going to find Matt and see if I can upsell him for the next issue. Good luck!" Katie walks away smirking, leaving me alone and a sitting duck. *Great*. I think about going after her, but I can't help but notice Dylan's also alone.

*Well, there's no time like the present.*

I blow out a deep breath, square my shoulders, and walk over to him. As I approach, he has the biggest smile I've ever seen—like a kid on Christmas morning. His boyish grin takes my breath away.

*What is wrong with me? You're here for work.*

I've never been so nervous to talk to someone before, but I muster up every ounce of courage I have, and draw from everything I learned in my public speaking and communications classes in college. *Deep breath, Em.*

"Dylan, hi." I offer a polite, flirty smile. If I have to talk to him, I may as well have some fun.

"Well, hello. Two nights in a row? Small world." Dylan brings his beer to his lips, still smiling. His eye contact is powerful but playful. "You mentioned last night that you work for a magazine. What do you do there?"

"I just started this month as an account executive, which is basically a fancy name for ad sales." I'm so nervous around him. Not only is he insanely attractive, he carries himself with so much confidence that I struggle to find my voice.

Dylan laughs, gesturing with his beer around the room. "Ah, yes, we have quite a few of those here. Which magazine? Do you have a card? I forgot to ask for it yesterday."

*Is he trying to get my number? No, that can't be it.*

I dig in my bag and pull one out. "Here, that's me."

Taking my card, he asks, "Is this the best number to reach you at?"

I stare for a moment, then clear my throat. "Um, yes, that's my work cell." I don't have a work cell, but he doesn't need to know that.

"Thanks." His smile meets his eyes as he pockets my card. "I'll have to give you a call when we are ready to put in an ad."

*Ugh, so it's a business thing. Damn it.*

To avoid his searing gaze, I use the only tool in my arsenal. "Sure thing. Well, it was great seeing you again, Dylan. Please excuse me." I hold up my phone that is most definitely *not* ringing. "I have to take this." I turn on my heel and walk away before I embarrass myself further.

With my phone to my ear, I look for Katie, willing myself not to sneak a glance at him as I retreat. I know damn well I'll find his ocean eyes on me. She's by the bar, laughing at something the guy she's with is saying. *What was his name? Mark? Michael?* I was too distracted by a tall drink of water with piercing blue eyes when she mentioned him to remember correctly.

"Oh, Emma! You must meet my absolute favorite client, Matt."

*Hah! I knew it was a M name.*

Shoving my phone in my bag, I extend my free hand to shake his, "Hi, Matt, it's a pleasure to meet you." Matt is in his mid-to-late twenties, tall and blond, but only a few inches taller than me in heels, putting him maybe six foot—which is a little shorter than Dylan. He's attractive, but not really my type. *Or maybe I'm just crushing on Dylan?*

He offers to grab me a glass of wine to replace the one I downed in one gulp on my way to find Katie, but I decline, "I'm okay, thank you. I just wanted to check in with Katie before I head out."

"Give me thirty and we can leave together?"

"Sure, I can wait for you," I reply as professionally as I can, but my nerves are shot. Just as I'm about to walk away, Dylan approaches, slapping Matt on the back to greet him, "Hey, buddy, how've you been?"

Matt chuckles. "Great, it's been a while! The office hasn't been the same since you transferred. Have you met Katie and... Emma, was it?"

As I'm about to confirm, Dylan replies for me with a wide grin, his dimples on full display, "Yes, we've met a few times. Old friends now, aren't we, E?"

*Shoot, now he wants to be just friends. That's worse than just business. I've been friend-zoned! Also, E? Since when do I have a nickname?*

He lowers his voice and leans in beside my ear so that only I can hear him. "When I call you, I hope you don't rush off the phone as quickly as you did with that one you took." I suck in a quick breath, unsure how to respond after being caught.

Katie jumps in, full of half-truths, "Emma was telling

me that she just took on five new clients. I don't know how she makes the time to join me at these events."

"Really, Katie?" I mutter under my breath.

Beaming, she continues, "Well, gentlemen, we have an early morning meeting that I forgot about, but I'm so glad we had a chance to catch up."

Dylan's smile fades. *Is he sad I'm leaving?* We shake hands and, the moment Dylan touches me, it feels like a mild electrical current travels up my arm. My hand fits perfectly in his and I appreciate that he doesn't offer a limp handshake like some men do, simply because I'm a woman. He pulls me a little closer, his thumb gently and ever so subtly swiping over mine.

*Did I imagine that?*

"I'm sure I'll see you soon, Emma." His voice is silky, and I have to remind myself that this is just work; he's probably like this with everyone.

Katie and I slip away from the crowd. Once we're out of earshot of everyone, she looks me dead in the eyes. "That man wants you. Time to play hard to get."

"I am *not* going to play hard to get," I insist. "Plus, he only wants to be friends or business acquaintances."

"Friends with benefits, maybe," Katie scoffs. "Did you see him checking you out as we left?" *Was he checking me out?* "Does he have your number?"

"He has my card."

"Mark my words, he wants more than a business relationship. Just be careful when he reaches out. By the way that man looks at you, he's probably the kind of guy who jumps in with two feet."

Katie's words replay in my head the entire way home.

# CHAPTER 2
## EMMA

In the last month since we first met, I've run into Dylan no less than ten more times. He sits at my table during every luncheon. Every mixer, he brings me a glass of wine or comes up with an excuse to talk to me. He *always* finds me. A few people have asked if we're dating —which is super awkward—but we always change the subject. The flirting is fun, but we're friends at best and business contacts at worst. I have no idea where we stand.

I'm in the middle of drafting an email to one of my clients when my cell phone rings with an unknown number. "Hello?"

"Hi, is this Emma?" The voice on the other line is familiar, but I can't place it.

"Yes, who's this?"

"Dylan," he says matter-of-factly, as if I should know who he is. Of course, I know *exactly* who he is, but I need to play it cool.

"Oh, hi, Dylan No-last-name," I tease. My voice feels shaky; I hope the quiver is only in my head. He lets out a hearty laugh.

"My apologies, I should've clarified. Dylan Alexander."

"Oh, hello." I clear my throat. "And how may I help you, Dylan Alexander?" I straighten my posture, even if no one can see it but me.

"I wanted to see if you were available to grab a drink or dinner to... discuss a few things."

*Like a friend thing? Or a business thing? Or a date thing?*

"Um, sure. I think I have a few evenings free but my lunches are all booked up." I'm a liar; I have zero lunches booked. *Ball's in your court, Dylan.* If this is a date, his next move should make it obvious.

"Perfect. How about Thursday evening, after work? Maybe 5 p.m.? I have a meeting that goes until five. Hope that's not too late?"

Well, shoot, his next move was *not* obvious. This could still be a work thing.

"Sure, that should be fine. My car will be at the train station, but I can grab it after work and meet you a little after 5:30?"

"That's not necessary. My meeting is downtown; I'll come pick you up."

*Oh my God, is this a date? No, there's no way, it still feels too stuffy.*

"Sure, my work address is on my card, I'll meet you downstairs when you're here," I reply. *What on earth is this man thinking?*

"Great, I'll see you then. You're sure you don't have plans?" It's an odd question for him to ask, I just told him I'm free.

"Nope, I'm available. See you Thursday."

"Can't wait." He hangs up, and I'm left gaping at my phone, wondering what the hell just happened.

---

Thursday comes quicker than I expected. When I look at my calendar, I realize why he double checked about my plans tonight—it's Valentine's Day. I still can't tell if this is a date or not, but I'm excited, no matter the outcome. I might walk away with a second date on the books, or a contract for an ad in the magazine. Win-win.

I make sure I'm downstairs a few minutes before five o'clock, surprised to discover he's right on time. Dylan pulls up to the building and gets out of his car to open my door for me. I don't know if it's possible, but is he even more handsome than I remember? I haven't seen him in a week, but it feels longer. Then, it hits me—he doesn't have a date tonight either.

On the drive to the restaurant, he asks me how my day was, and I ask about his. He rattles off some sort of stock trading information that I barely follow. So far, this outing feels very platonic. He didn't comment on how pretty I look, or do any other complimentary first date things guys typically do. I'm starting to think I read this all wrong. Maybe he's just not that into me and it's all business.

We decided to eat at a local seafood restaurant that, in my opinion, is casual enough to grab dinner as a date, but fancy enough to buy him dinner if it's a business meeting. I still have no clue what this is and suggested eating here to be sure I'm covered either way.

Entering the restaurant, the host seats us at a table in the middle of the room. Dylan sits across from me, and damn it, now I can't avoid his dimples.

As the waiter asks my drink order, I reply, "Gin and tonic with extra lime, please."

I set my napkin on my lap and look up to find Dylan with a curious expression. He pauses for a moment, his trademark dimples bigger than ever. Shaking his head with a smirk, he turns to the server. "Make that two, please." Once they leave, I ask Dylan what his look was for. He laughs to himself and replies, "Nothing. You just surprise me." I smile back, feeling a little like he's flirting with me.

There's a shift between us once we order dinner; almost all the questions he asks me are personal, like he wants to know *me*. Nothing about work. Halfway done with my drink, I decide it's time to put on my big girl panties and ask what I've been wondering all evening, "I hope you don't take this the wrong way, I just don't want to misread the situation. Is this a business dinner, or is this... *a date?*"

I bite my lower lip, awaiting his response, which feels like eternity—even if it's only a few seconds. "You're right. I'm sorry I wasn't clear with my intentions. I was actually hoping it would be a date. But if you prefer we keep things professional, I completely respect that."

"Well, I was planning on discussing potential advertising over drinks; my treat, of course. But I would be more than okay if this was a date instead." I feel a blush creeping up my neck to my cheeks.

As if his smile couldn't get any wider, I swear it just did. I've never met a man who looks at a woman the way he's looking at me. It's something movies are made of. Maybe Katie was right all along, and it was actually the perfect meet cute.

"So, to be clear, putting an ad in our magazine is *not* something you want to do?" I jest, as I continue to slowly sip my drink. I should look away, but I can't bring myself to end this staredown.

He quietly replies into his glass, "There are at least thirty things I want to do with you, and that *definitely* isn't one of them."

I nearly spit out my gin and tonic. At first, I'm not sure I heard him properly, but his eyes darken as he watches me.

*Oof, this guy is trouble.*

"So, tell me, when was the last time you went to a base-ball game?"

I appreciate him changing the subject, the flirting is making it way too hot in here. *It's hot in here, right?* "I haven't been in a while but used to have season tickets down in San Diego when I was younger."

His boyish grin returns and my guess is he loves baseball as much as I do. "We should go sometime when they're playing up here."

"Getting ahead of ourselves, are we, Mr. Alexander? For all you know, tonight could be the date from hell, and I'll never want to see you again." I'm having way too much fun teasing him, but I swear I heard him exhale a groan when I called him that. *Interesting.*

"You and I both know how this is going to go." He's so confident, but there's so much truth to his words; I've been inexplicably drawn to him since the moment we met.

The rest of dinner is filled with laughter and "get to know you" conversation. Sadly, he brought the flirting down a notch, but I've enjoyed learning more about him. He's driven and one of the youngest in his line of business, which I relate to—being twenty-one and up for promotion after only working at the magazine for a month.

When we finish eating, he drives me back to the office; I need to grab my laptop upstairs before I head to the train station across the street. My hand moves to the handle to open the car door, but he stops me with his hand on my thigh. I suck in a breath. When I look at him, he shakes his head. "Don't you dare. That's my job." I smile at the chivalry, even if my body is on fire.

Once we're both out of the car, I know this is the moment that will make or break us. If he's an amazing kisser, I'm a goner. If he's a horrible kisser, I don't know if I can save face seeing him at events. There's something about him, though. I have a feeling it's going to be the former.

He steps toward me and takes my hand, gently caressing his thumb on top of mine. "I had an amazing time tonight." He tucks my hair behind my ear and I'm screaming inside.

"I did, too." I wet my lips in anticipation. There's a quiet moment between us before he leans forward and I lift my heels to meet him halfway until our lips meet. The kiss is soft, gentle, but I sense he is holding back. It isn't the fireworks I was anticipating, and it isn't an epic earth-shattering kiss from my favorite books, but the flutter in my stomach is undeniable.

He steps back and opens the door to my office building for me to walk through. "Have a great rest of your night."

*That's it? That's all I get?*

I sigh. "You as well." I walk into my building, looking back for a moment to watch him return to his car. Maybe it was all in my head, but the chemistry I have with him is like nothing I've ever felt. I can't help feeling a little disappointed he let me go easily.

About twenty minutes later, there's a text as I'm boarding the commuter train. My heart stops when I see it's him.

DYLAN

I know your team isn't playing, but will
you join me for a game Saturday night?

*Butterflies, settle down!*

I can't wait for Saturday.

# ACKNOWLEDGMENTS

First, I would like to thank my dear friend and critique partner, Amanda. "You're more beautiful than Cinderella, you smell like pine needles and your face is like sunshine."

To my alpha readers Whisper, Lakshmi, Lo, Kel, Jamie, and Jessica — You ladies are amazing! I'm so grateful for all of your help with this book.

To my ARC readers — Thanks for taking a chance on me! I know my books are so different from other spicy romcoms, so thank you for jumping in with two feet. I am so blessed to have all of you reading and reviewing my work before launch.

To my incredible line editor H.M. Darling — Without you, my books would be trash! I can't thank you enough for helping make my book amazing!

To my friend Ellie — Hope one day you'll have a chance to get Handsy at Hamilton.

To my friend Wolf — Who knew that too many takes of "good girl" would inspire a whole damn book? Thank you for your patience and being such a cool fucking person.

Finally, thank you to all of my author friends for not letting my imposter syndrome take over, my "real life" friends for believing in me, and my family for putting up with my silly little dream of becoming a published author.

xoxo,

Irene

## ABOUT IRENE

Irene Bahrd is a Gryffindor Capricorn and one of the most avid readers you'll ever meet.

She started her writing journey as a dare from a friend, after recounting dating stories from her early twenties. They inspired her to write spicy parody and romantic comedy novels that feature a variety of book boyfriends —from growly alpha heroes to cinnamon roll golden retrievers.

Her favorite genres to read include fantasy romance and contemporary dark romance. You'll find some of her favorite books and authors referenced by characters in her own books.

Irene can be found on Instagram and TikTok under @irenebahrdauthor

## ALSO BY IRENE BAHRD

**Love at all Cost Series**

A Voice Without Reason

Not Her Villain

Maybe in Fifty *(Prequel Novella to Unexpectedly Ruined)*

Unexpectedly Ruined

Sip Happens *(Novella)*

**Top Shelf Romances Series**

Mine with Extra Lime

Falling the Old Fashioned Way

Royally on the Rocks

Trouble with a Twist

**Top Shelf Novellas**

Wine About It

Rosé to the Occasion

Mule Tide Cheer

**Love & Politics Series**

Arranged Vacancy

**Sapphire Lake Series**

Never Yours

**Expect the Unexpected Parody Novella Duet**

Undeclared Heir

Undecided Heiress

**Pelligini Crime Daddies Parody Novella Duet**

Running from the Garden with Eden

Not My Bodyguard's Keeper

## Magical Mischief Parody Novella Series

Unshifted

Uncharmed

## Holiday ErotiCom Novella Series

Merry in Spite

ForNever Mine

Summer of the Switch

Haunted Happenstance

Save a Horse

## Stand Alone ErotiComs

Flexible Standards

The Al Dente Diet *(Collaboration with J.L. Quick)*

## Thirst Trap Book Boyfriends Satire Series

Trapp Temptations: Vol. 1

Trapp Temptations: Vol. 2

www.ingramcontent.com/pod-product-compliance
Lightning Source LLC
Chambersburg PA
CBHW060355260626
47160CB00006B/2314